ABOUT THE AUTHOR

"The Stratemeyer Syndicate is fascinating because of how many well-known series they created under several pen identities, such Victor Appleton. The most well-known series published under the Victor Appleton identity is Tom Swift, and like the other series ""authored"" by Victor Appleton, the plots for this one were created from outlines by ghostwriters. A second series was created because Tom Swift was so well-liked. The Syndicate determined in 1954 that the first series' Tom Swift had a teenage son who emulated his father's inventiveness. Compared to the first series, this second one has more space-related themes (which featured airships and other inventions appropriate to its time period). Victor Appleton II, the author's son who was created in the same way as Tom Swift was, was not a real-life person like the original pen name Victor Appleton."

TOM SWIFT AND HIS AERIAL WARSHIP;
OR,
THE NAVAL TERROR OF THE SEAS

By

VICTOR APPLETON

Tom Swift And His Aerial Warship; Or,
The Naval Terror of the Seas

by Victor Appleton

ISBN: 978-93-57482-98-1

Published by

DOUBLE 9 BOOKS

2/13-B, Ansari Road
Daryaganj, New Delhi – 110002
info@double9books.com
www.double9books.com
Tel. 011-40042856

CONTENTS

CHAPTER I   TOM IS PUZZLED...7

CHAPTER II   A FIRE ALARM.. 12

CHAPTER III   A DESPERATE BATTLE... 17

CHAPTER IV   SUSPICIONS.. 22

CHAPTER V   A QUEER STRANGER 27

CHAPTER VI   THE AERIAL WARSHIP 33

CHAPTER VII   WARNINGS.. 39

CHAPTER VIII   A SUSPECTED PLOT 45

CHAPTER IX   THE RECOIL CHECK 49

CHAPTER X   THE NEW MEN... 54

CHAPTER XI   A DAY OFF... 59

CHAPTER XII   A NIGHT ALARM 65

CHAPTER XIII   THE CAPTURE 70

CHAPTER XIV   THE FIRST FLIGHT 74

CHAPTER XV   IN DANGER 79

CHAPTER XVI   TOM IS WORRIED.. 84

CHAPTER XVII   AN OCEAN FLIGHT 89

CHAPTER XVIII   IN A STORM.. 95

CHAPTER XIX   QUEER HAPPENINGS 100

CHAPTER XX   THE STOWAWAYS.. 104

CHAPTER XXI   PRISONERS.. 109

CHAPTER XXII   APPREHENSIONS.. 113

CHAPTER XXIII   ACROSS THE SEA 117

CHAPTER XXIV   THE LIGHTNING BOLT.. 120

CHAPTER XXV   FREEDOM.. 125

CHAPTER I
TOM IS PUZZLED

"What's the matter, Tom? You look rather blue!"

"Blue! Say, Ned, I'd turn red, green, yellow, or any other color of the rainbow, if I thought it would help matters any."

"Whew!"

Ned Newton, the chum and companion of Tom Swift, gave vent to a whistle of surprise, as he gazed at the young fellow sitting opposite him, near a bench covered with strange-looking tools and machinery, while blueprints and drawings were scattered about.

Ranged on the sides of the room were models of many queer craft, most of them flying machines of one sort or another, while through the open door that led into a large shed could be seen the outlines of a speedy monoplane.

"As bad as that, eh, Tom?" went on Ned. "I thought something was up when I first came in, but, if you'll excuse a second mention of the color scheme, I should say it was blue—decidedly blue. You look as though you had lost your last friend, and I want to assure you that if you do feel that way, it's dead wrong. There's myself, for one, and I'm sure Mr. Damon—"

"Bless my gasoline tank!" exclaimed Tom, with a laugh, in imitation of the gentleman Ned Newton had mentioned, "I know that! I'm not worrying over the loss of any friends."

"And there are Eradicate, and Koku, the giant, just to mention a couple of others," went on Ned, with a smile.

"That's enough!" exclaimed Tom. "It isn't that, I tell you."

"Well, what is it then? Here I go and get a half-holiday off from the bank, and just at the busiest time, too, to come and see you, and I find you in a brown study, looking as blue as indigo, and maybe you're all yellow inside from a bilious attack, for all I know."

"Quite a combination of colors," admitted Tom. "But it isn't what you think. It's just that I'm puzzled, Ned."

"Puzzled?" and Ned raised his eyebrows to indicate how surprised he was that anything should puzzle his friend.

"Yes, genuinely puzzled."

"Has anything gone wrong?" Ned asked. "No one is trying to take any of your pet inventions away from you, is there?"

"No, not exactly that, though it is about one of my inventions I am puzzled. I guess I haven't shown you my very latest; have I, Ned?"

"Well, I don't know, Tom. Time was when I could keep track of you and your inventions, but that was in your early days, when you started with a motorcycle and were glad enough to have a motorboat. But, since you've taken to aerial navigation and submarine work, not to mention one or two other lines of activity, I give up. I don't know where to look next, Tom, for something new."

"Well, this isn't so very new," went on the young inventor, for Tom Swift had designed and patented many new machines of the air, earth and water. "I'm just trying to work out some new problems in aerial navigation, Ned," he went on.

"I thought there weren't any more," spoke Ned, soberly enough.

"Come, now, none of that!" exclaimed Tom, with a laugh. "Why, the surface of aerial navigation has only been scratched. The science is far from being understood, or even made safe, not to say perfected, as water and land travel have been. There's lots of chance yet."

"And you're working on something new?" asked Ned, as he looked around the shop where he and Tom were sitting. As the young bank employee had said, he had come away from the institution that afternoon to have a little holiday with his chum, but Tom, seated in the midst of his inventions, seemed little inclined to jollity.

Through the open windows came the hum of distant machinery, for Tom Swift and his father were the heads of a company founded to manufacture and market their many inventions, and about their home were grouped several buildings. From a small plant the business had grown to be a great tree, under the direction of Tom and his father.

"Yes, I'm working on something new," admitted Tom, after a moment of silence.

"And, Ned," he went on, "there's no reason why you shouldn't see it. I've been keeping it a bit secret, until I had it a little further advanced, but I've got to a point now where I'm stuck, and perhaps it will do me good to talk to someone about it."

"Not to talk to me, though, I'm afraid. What I don't know about machinery, Tom, would fill a great many books. I don't see how I can help you," and Ned laughed.

"Well, perhaps you can, just the same, though you may not know a lot of technical things about machines. It sometimes helps me just to tell my troubles to a disinterested person, and hear him ask questions. I've got dad half distracted trying to solve the problem, so I've had to let up on him for a while. Come on out and see what you make of it."

"Sure, Tom, anything to oblige. If you want me to sit in front of your photo-telephone, and have my picture taken, I'm agreeable, even if you shoot off a flashlight at my ear. Or, if you want me to see how long I can stay under water without breathing I'll try that, too, provided you don't leave me under too long, lead the way—I'm agreeable as far as I'm able, old man."

"Oh, it isn't anything like that," Tom answered with a laugh. "I might as well give you a few hints, so you'll know what I'm driving at. Then I'll take you out and show it to you."

"What is it—air, earth or water?" asked Ned Newton, for he knew his chum's activities led along all three lines.

"This happens to be air."

"A new balloon?"

"Something like that. I call it my aerial warship, though."

"Aerial warship, Tom! That sounds rather dangerous!"

"It will be dangerous, too, if I can get it to work. That's what it's intended for."

"But a warship of the air!" cried Ned. "You can't mean it. A warship carries guns, mortars, bombs, and—"

"Yes, I know," interrupted Tom, "and I appreciate all that when I called my newest craft an aerial warship."

"But," objected Ned, "an aircraft that will carry big guns will be so large that—"

"Oh, mine is large enough," Tom broke in.

"Then it's finished!" cried Ned eagerly, for he was much interested in his chum's inventions.

"Well, not exactly," Tom said. "But what I was going to tell you was that all guns are not necessarily large. You can get big results with small guns and projectiles now, for high-powered explosives come in small packages. So it isn't altogether a question of carrying a certain amount of weight. Of course, an aerial warship will have to be big, for it will have to carry extra machinery to give it extra speed, and it will have to carry a certain armament, and a large crew will be needed. So, as I said, it will need to be large. But that problem isn't worrying me."

"Well, what is it, then?" asked Ned.

"It's the recoil," said Tom, with a gesture of despair.

"The recoil?" questioned Ned, wonderingly.

"Yes, from the guns, you know. I haven't been able to overcome that, and, until I do, I'm afraid my latest invention will be a failure."

Ned shook his head.

"I'm afraid I can't help you any," he said. "The only thing I know about recoils is connected with an old shotgun my father used to own.

"I took that once, when he didn't know it," Ned proceeded. "It was pretty heavily loaded, for the crows had been having fun in our cornfield, and dad had been shooting at them. This time I thought I'd take a chance.

"Well, I fired the gun. But it must have had a double charge in it and been rusted at that. All I know is that after I pulled the trigger I thought the end of the world had come. I heard a clap of thunder, and then I went flying over backward into a blackberry patch."

"That was the recoil," said Tom.

"The what?" asked Ned.

"The recoil. The recoil of the gun knocked you over."

"Oh, yes," observed Ned, rubbing his shoulder in a reflective sort of way. "I always thought it was something like that. But, at the time I put it down to an explosion, and let it go at that."

"No, it wasn't an explosion, properly speaking," said Tom. "You see, when powder explodes, in a gun, or otherwise, its force is exerted in all directions, up, down and every way."

"This went mostly backward—in my direction," said Ned ruefully.

"You only thought so," returned Tom. "Most of the power went out in front, to force out the shot. Part of it, of course, was exerted on the barrel of the gun—that was sideways—but the strength of the steel held it in. And part of the force went backward against your shoulder. That part was the recoil, and it is the recoil of the guns I figure on putting aboard my aerial warship that is giving me such trouble."

"Is that what makes you look so blue?" asked Ned.

"That's it. I can't seem to find a way by which to take up the recoil, and the force of it, from all the guns I want to carry, will just about tear my ship to pieces, I figure."

"Then you haven't actually tried it out yet?" asked Ned.

"Not the guns, no. I have the warship of the air nearly done, but I've worked out on paper the problem of the guns far enough so that I know I'm up against it. It can't be done, and an aerial warship without guns wouldn't be worth much, I'm afraid."

"I suppose not," agreed Ned. "And is it only the recoil that is bothering you?"

"Mostly. But come, take a look at my latest pet," and Tom arose to lead the way to another shed, a large one in the distance, toward which he waved his hand to indicate to his chum that there was housed the wonderful invention.

The two chums crossed the yard, threading their way through the various buildings, until they stood in front of the structure to which Tom had called attention.

"It's in here," he said. "I don't mind admitting that I'm quite proud of it, Ned; that is, proud as far as I've gone. But the gun business sure has me worried. I'm going to talk it off on you. Hello!" cried Tom suddenly, as he put a key in the complicated lock on the door, "someone has been in here. I wonder who it is?"

Ned was a little startled at the look on Tom's face and the sound of alarm in his chum's voice.

CHAPTER II
A FIRE ALARM

Tom Swift quickly opened the door of the big shed. It was built to house a dirigible balloon, or airship of some sort. Ned could easily tell that from his knowledge of Tom's previous inventions.

"Something wrong?" asked the young bank clerk.

"I don't know," returned Tom, and then as he looked inside the place, he breathed a sigh of relief.

"Oh, it's you, is it, Koku?" he asked, as a veritable giant of a man came forward.

"Yes, master, it is only Koku and your father," spoke the big chap, with rather a strange accent.

"Oh, is my father here?" asked Tom. "I was wondering who had opened the door of this shed."

"Yes, Tom," responded the elder Swift, coming up to them, "I had a new idea in regard to some of those side guy wires, and I wanted to try it out. I brought Koku with me to use his strength on some of them."

"That's all right, Dad. Ned and I came out to wrestle with that recoil problem again. I want to try some guns on the craft soon, but—"

"You'd better not, Tom," warned his father. "It will never work, I tell you. You can't expect to take up quick-firing guns and bombs in an airship, and have them work properly. Better give it up."

"I never will. I'll make it work, Dad!"

"I don't believe you will, Tom. This time you have bitten off more than you can chew, to use a homely but expressive statement."

"Well, Dad, we'll see," began Tom easily. "There she is, Ned," he went on. "Now, if you'll come around here..."

But Tom never finished that sentence, for at that moment there came running into the airship shed an elderly, short, stout, fussy gentleman, followed by an aged colored man. Both of them seemed very much excited.

"Bless my socks, Tom!" cried the short, stout man. "There sure is trouble!"

"I should say So, Massa Tom!" added the colored man. "I done did prognosticate dat some day de combustible material of which dat shed am composed would conflaggrate—"

"What's the matter?" interrupted Tom, jumping forward. "Speak out! Eradicate! Mr. Damon, what is it?"

"The red shed!" cried the short little man. "The red shed, Tom!"

"It's on fire!" yelled the colored man.

"Great thunderclaps!" cried Tom. "Come on—everybody on the job!" he yelled. "Koku, pull the alarm! If that red shed goes—"

Instantly the place was in confusion. Tom and Ned, looking from a window of the hangar, saw a billow of black smoke roll across the yard. But already the private fire bell was clanging out its warning. And, while the work of fighting the flames is under way, I will halt the progress of this story long enough to give my new readers a little idea of who Tom Swift is, so they may read this book more intelligently. Those of you who have perused the previous volumes may skip this part.

Tom Swift, though rather young in years, was an inventor of note. His tastes and talents were developed along the line of machinery and locomotion. Motorcycles, automobiles, motorboats, submarine craft, and, latest of all, craft of the air, had occupied the attention of Tom Swift and his father for some years.

Mr. Swift was a widower, and lived with Tom, his only son, in the village of Shopton, New York State. Mrs. Baggert kept house for them, and an aged colored man, Eradicate Sampson, with his mule, Boomerang, did "odd jobs" about the Shopton home and factories.

Among Tom's friends was a Mr. Wakefield Damon, from a nearby village. Mr. Damon was always blessing something, from his hat to his shoes, a harmless sort of habit that seemed to afford him much comfort. Then there was Ned Newton, a boyhood chum of Tom's, who worked in the Shopton bank. I will just mention Mary Nestor, a young lady of Shopton, in whom Tom was more than ordinarily interested. I have spoken of Koku, the giant. He really was a giant of a man, of enormous strength, and was one of two whom

Tom had brought with him from a strange land where Tom was held captive for a time. You may read about it in a book devoted to those adventures.

Tom took Koku into his service, somewhat to the dismay of Eradicate, who was desperately jealous. But poor Eradicate was getting old, and could not do as much as he thought he could. So, in a great measure, Koku replaced him, and Tom found much use for the giant's strength.

Tom had begun his inventive work when, some years before this story opens, he had bargained for Mr. Damon's motorcycle, after that machine had shot its owner into a tree. Mr. Damon was, naturally, perhaps, much disgusted, and sold the affair cheap. Tom repaired it, made some improvements, and, in the first volume of this series, entitled "Tom Swift and His Motor-cycle," you may read of his rather thrilling adventures on his speedy road-steed.

From then on Tom had passed a busy life, making many machines and having some thrilling times with them. Just previous to the opening of this story Tom had made a peculiar instrument, described in the volume entitled "Tom Swift and His Photo-Telephone." With that a person talking could not only see the features of the person with whom he was conversing, but, by means of a selenium plate and a sort of camera, a permanent picture could be taken of the person at either end of the wire.

By means of this invention Tom had been able to make a picture that had saved a fortune. But Tom did not stop there. With him to invent was as natural and necessary as breathing. He simply could not stop it. And so we find him now about to show to his chum, Ned Newton, his latest patent, an aerial warship, which, however, was not the success Tom had hoped for.

But just at present other matters than the warship were in Tom's mind. The red shed was on fire.

That mere statement might not mean anything special to the ordinary person, but to Tom, his father, and those who knew about his shops, it meant much.

"The red shed!" Tom cried. "We mustn't let that get the best of us! Everybody at work! Father, not you, though. You mustn't excite yourself!"

Even in the midst of the alarm Tom thought of his father, for the aged man had a weak heart, and had on one occasion nearly expired, being saved just in time by the arrival of a doctor, whom Tom brought to the scene after a wonderful race through the air.

"But, Tom, I can help," objected the aged inventor.

"Now, you just take care of yourself, Father!" Tom cried. "There are enough of us to look after this fire, I think."

"But, Tom, it—it's the red shed!" gasped Mr. Swift.

"I realize that, Dad. But it can't have much of a start yet. Is the alarm ringing, Koku?"

"Yes, Master," replied the giant, in correct but stilted English. "I have set the indicator to signal the alarm in every shop on the premises."

"That's right." Tom sprang toward the door. "Eradicate!" he called.

"Yais, sah! Heah I is!" answered the colored man. "I'll go git mah mule, Boomerang, right away, an' he—"

"Don't you bring Boomerang on the scene!" Tom yelled. "When I want that shed kicked apart I can do it better than by using a mule's heels. And you know you can't do a thing with Boomerang when he sees fire."

"Now dat's so, Massa Tom. But I could put blinkers on him, an'—"

"No, you let Boomerang stay where he is. Come on, Ned. We'll see what we can do. Mr. Damon—"

"Yes, Tom, I'm right here," answered the peculiar man, for he had come over from his home in Waterford to pay a visit to his friends, Tom and Mr. Swift. "I'll do anything I can to help you, Tom, bless my necktie!" he went on. "Only say the word!"

"We've got to get some of the stuff out of the place!" Tom cried. "We may be able to save it, but I can't take a chance on putting out the fire and letting some of the things in there go up in smoke. Come on!"

Those in the shed where was housed what Tom hoped would prove to be a successful aerial warship rushed to the open. From the other shops and buildings nearby were pouring men and boys, for the Swift plant employed a number of hands now.

Above the shouts and yells, above the crackle of flames, could be heard the clanging of the alarm bell, set ringing by Koku, who had pulled the signal in the airship shed. From there it had gone to every building in the plant, being relayed by the telephone operator, whose duty it was to look after that.

"My, you've got a big enough fire-fighting force, Tom!" cried Ned in his chum's ear.

"Yes, I guess we can master it, if it hasn't gotten the best of us. Say, it's going some, though!"

Tom pointed to where a shed, painted red—a sign of danger—could be seen partly enveloped in smoke, amid the black clouds of which shot out red tongues of flame.

"What have you got it painted red for?" Ned asked pantingly, as they ran on.

"Because—" Tom began, but the rest of the sentence was lost in a yell.

Tom had caught sight of Eradicate and the giant, Koku, unreeling from a central standpipe a long line of hose.

"Don't take that!" Tom cried. "Don't use that hose! Drop it!"

"What's the matter? Is it rotten?" Ned wanted to know.

"No, but if they pull it out the water will be turned on automatically."

"Well, isn't that what you want at a fire—water?" Ned demanded.

"Not at this fire," was Tom's answer. "There's a lot of calcium carbide in that red shed—that's why it's red—to warn the men of danger. You know what happens when water gets on carbide—there's an explosion, and there's enough carbide in that shed to send the whole works sky high.

"Drop that hose!" yelled Tom in louder tones. "Drop it, Rad—Koku! Do you want to kill us all!"

CHAPTER III
A DESPERATE BATTLE

Tom's tones and voice were so insistent that the giant and the colored man had no choice but to obey. They dropped the hose which, half unreeled, lay like some twisted snake in the grass. Had it been pulled out all the way the water would have spurted from the nozzle, for it was of the automatic variety, with which Tom had equipped all his plant.

"But what are you going to do, Tom, if you don't use water?" asked Ned, wonderingly.

"I don't know—yet, but I know water is the worst thing you can put on carbide," returned Tom. For all he spoke Slowly his brain was working fast. Already, even now, he was planning how best to give battle to the flames.

It needed but an instant's thought on the part of Ned to make him understand that Tom was right. It would be well-nigh fatal to use water on carbide. Those of you who have bicycle lanterns, in which that not very pleasant-smelling chemical is used, know that if a few drops of water are allowed to drip slowly on the gray crystals acetylene gas is generated, which makes a brilliant light. But, if the water drips too fast, the gas is generated too quickly, and an explosion results. In lamps, of course, and in lighting plants where carbide is used, there are automatic arrangements to prevent the water flowing too freely to the chemical. But Tom knew if the hose were turned on the fire in the red shed a great explosion would result, for some of the tins of carbide would be melted by the heat.

Yet the fire needed to be coped with. Already the flames were coming through the roof, and the windows and door were spouting red fire and volumes of smoke.

Several other employees of Tom's plant had made ready to unreel more hose, but the warning of the young inventor, shouted to Eradicate and Koku, had had its effect. Every man dropped the line he had begun to unreel.

"Ha! Massa Tom say drop de hose, but how yo' gwine t' squirt watah on a fire wifout a hose; answer me dat?" and Eradicate looked at Koku.

"Me no know," was the slow answer. "I guess Koku go pull shed down and stamp out fire."

"Huh! Maybe yo' could do dat in cannibal land, where yo' all come from," spoke Eradicate, "but yo' can't do dat heah! 'Sides, de red shed will blow up soon. Dere's suffin' else in dere except carbide, an' dat's gwine t' go up soon, dat's suah!"

"Maybe you get your strong man-mule, Boomerang," suggested Koku. "Nothing ever hurt him—explosion or nothing. He can kick shed all to pieces, and put out fire."

"Dat's what I wanted t' do, but Massa Tom say I cain't," explained the colored man. "Golly! Look at dat fire!"

Indeed the blaze was now assuming alarming proportions. The red shed, which was not a small structure, was blazing on all sides. About it stood the men from the various shops.

"Tom, you must do something," said Mr. Swift. "If the flames once reach that helmanite—"

"I know, Father. But that explosive is in double vacuum containers, and it will be safe for some time yet. Besides, it's in the cellar. It's the carbide I'm most worried about. We daren't use water."

"But something will have to be done!" exclaimed Mr. Damon. "Bless my red necktie, if we don't—"

"Better get back a way," suggested Tom. "Something may go off!"

His words of warning had their effect, and the whole circle moved back several paces.

"Is there anything of value in the shed?" asked Ned.

"I should say there was!" Tom answered. "I hoped we could get some of them out, but we can't now—until the fire dies down a bit, at any rate."

"Look, Tom! The pattern shop roof is catching!" shouted Mr. Swift, pointing to where a little spurt of flame showed on the roof of a distant building.

"It's from sparks!" Tom said.

"Any danger of using water there?" Ned wanted to know.

"No, use all you like! That's the only thing to do. Come on, you with the hose!" Tom yelled. "Save the other buildings!"

"But are you going to let the red shed burn?" asked Mr. Swift. "You know what it means, Tom."

"Yes, Father, I know. And I'm going to fight that fire in a new way. But we must save the other buildings, too. Play water on all the other sheds and structures!" ordered the young inventor. "I'll tackle this one myself. Oh, Ned!" he called.

"Yes," answered his chum. "What is it?"

"You take charge of protecting the place where the new aerial warship is stored. Will you? I can't afford to lose that."

"I'll look after it, Tom. No harm in using water there, though; is there?"

"Not if you don't use too much. Some of the woodwork isn't varnished yet, and I wouldn't want it to be wet. But do the best you can. Take Koku and Eradicate with you. They can't do any good here."

"Do you mean to say you're going to give up and let this burn?"

"Not a bit of it, Ned. But I have another plan I want to try. Lively now! The wind's changing, and it's blowing over toward my aerial warship shed. If that catches—"

Tom shook his head protestingly, and Ned set off on the run, calling to the colored man and the giant to get out another line of hose.

"I wonder what Tom is going to do?" mused Ned, as he neared the big shed he and the others had left on the alarm of fire.

Tom, himself, seemed in no doubt as to his procedure. With one look at the blazing red shed, as if to form an opinion as to how much longer it could burn without getting entirely beyond control, Tom set off on a run toward another large structure. Ned, glancing toward his chum, observed:

"The dirigible shed! I wonder what his game is? Surely that can't be in danger—it's too far off!"

Ned was right as to the last statement. The shed, where was housed a great dirigible balloon Tom had made, but which he seldom used of late, was sufficiently removed from the zone of fire to be out of danger.

Meanwhile several members of the fire-fighting force that had been summoned from the various shops by the alarm, had made an effort to save from the red shed some of the more valuable of the contents. There were some machines in there, as well as explosives and chemicals, in addition to the store of carbide.

But the fire was now too hot to enable much to be done in the way of salvage. One or two small things were carried out from a little addition to the main structure, and then the rescuers were driven back by the heat of the flames, as well as by the rolling clouds of black smoke.

"Keep away!" warned Mr. Swift. "It will explode soon. Keep back!"

"That's right!" added Mr. Damon. "Bless my powder-horn! We may all be going sky-high soon, and without aid from any of Tom Swift's aeroplanes, either."

Warned by the aged inventor, the throng of men began slowly moving away from the immediate neighborhood of the blazing shed. Though it may seem to the reader that some time has elapsed since the first sounding of the alarm, all that I have set down took place in a very short period—hardly three minutes elapsing since Tom and the others came rushing out of the aerial warship building.

Suddenly a cry arose from the crowd of men near the red shed. Ned, who stood ready with several lines of hose, in charge of Koku, Eradicate and others, to turn them on the airship shed, in case of need, looked in the direction of the excited throng.

The young bank clerk saw a strange sight. From the top of the dirigible balloon shed a long, black, cigar-shaped body arose, floating gradually upward. The very roof of the shed slid back out of the way, as Tom pressed the operating lever, and the dirigible was free to rise—as free as though it had been in an open field.

"He's going up!" cried Ned in surprise. "Making an ascent at a time like this, when he ought to stay here to fight the fire! What's gotten into Tom, I'd like to know? I wonder if he can be—"

Ned did not finish his half-formed sentence. A dreadful thought came into his mind. What if the sudden fire, and the threatened danger, as well as the prospective loss that confronted Tom, had affected his mind?

"It certainly looks so," mused Ned, as he saw the big balloon float free from the shed. There was no doubt but that Tom was in it. He could be seen standing within the pilot-house, operating the various wheels and levers that controlled the ship of the air.

"What can he be up to?" marveled Ned. "Is he going to run away from the fire?"

Koku, Eradicate and several others were attracted by the sight of the great dirigible, now a considerable distance up in the air. Certainly it looked as though Tom Swift were running away. Yet Ned knew his chum better than that.

Then, as they watched, Ned and the others saw the direction of the balloon change. She turned around in response to the influence of the rudders and propellers, and was headed straight for the blazing shed, but some distance above it.

"What can he be planning?" wondered Ned.

He did not have long to wait to find out.

An instant later Tom's plan was made clear to his chum. He saw Tom circling over the burning red shed, and then the bank clerk saw what looked like fine rain dropping from the lower part of the balloon straight into the flames.

"He can't be dousing water on from up above there," reasoned Ned. "Pouring water on carbide from a height is just as bad as spurting it on from a hose, though perhaps not so dangerous to the persons doing it. But it can't be—"

"By Jove!" suddenly exclaimed Ned, as he had a better view of what was going on. "It's sand, that's what it is! Tom is giving battle to the flames with sand from the ballast bags of the dirigible! Hurray? That's the ticket! Sand! The only thing safe to use in case of an explosive chemical fire.

"Fine for you. Tom Swift! Fine!"

CHAPTER IV
SUSPICIONS

High up aloft, over the blazing red shed, with its dangerous contents that any moment might explode, Tom Swift continued to hold his big dirigible balloon as near the flames as possible. And as he stood outside on the small deck in front of the pilot-house, where were located the various controls, the young inventor pulled the levers that emptied bag after bag of fine sand on the spouting flames that, already, were beginning to die down as a result of this effectual quenching.

"Tom's done the trick!" yelled Ned, paying little attention now to the big airship shed, since he saw that the danger was about over.

"Dhat's what he suah hab done!" agreed Eradicate. "Mah ole mule Boomerang couldn't 'a' done any better."

"Huh! Your mule afraid of fire," remarked Koku.

"What's dat? Mah mule afraid ob fire?" cried the colored man. "Look heah, yo' great, big, overgrowed specimen ob an equilateral quadruped, I'll hab yo' all understand dat when yo' all speaks dat way about a friend ob mine dat yo'—"

"That'll do, Rad!" broke in Ned, with a laugh. He knew that when Tom's helper grew excited on the subject of his mule there was no stopping him, and Boomerang was a point on which Eradicate and Koku were always arguing. "The fire is under control now."

"Yes, it seems to have gone visiting," observed Koku.

"Visiting?" queried Ned, in some surprise.

"Yes, that is, it is going out," went on Koku.

"Oh, I understand!" laughed Ned. "Yes, and I hope it doesn't pay us another visit soon. Oh, look at Tom, would you!" he cried, for the young aviator had swung his ship about over the flames, to bring another row of sand bags directly above a place where the fire was hottest.

Down showered more sand from the bags which Tom opened. No fire could long continue to blaze under that treatment. The supply of air was cut off, and without that no fire can exist. Water would have been worse than useless, because of the carbide, but the sand covered it up so that it was made perfectly harmless.

Moving slowly, the airship hovered over every part of the now slowly expiring flames, the burned opening in the roof of the shed making it possible for the sand to reach the spots where it was most needed. The flames died out in section after section, until no more could be seen—only clouds of black smoke.

"How is it now?" came Tom's voice, as he spoke from the deck of the balloon through a megaphone.

"Almost out," answered Mr. Damon. "A little more sand, Tom."

The eccentric man had caught up a piece of paper and, rolling it into a cone, made an improvised megaphone of that.

"Haven't much more sand left," was Tom's comment, as he sent down a last shower. "That will have to do. Hustle that carbide and other explosive stuff out of there now, while you have a chance."

"That's it!" cried Ned, who caught his chums meaning. "Come on, Koku. There's work for you."

"Me like work," answered the giant, stretching out his great arms.

The last of the sand had completely smothered the fire, and Tom, observing from aloft that his work was well done, moved away in the dirigible, sending it to a landing space some little distance away from the shed whence it had arisen. It was impossible to drop it back again through the roof of the hangar, as the balloon was of such bulk that even a little breeze would deflect it so that it could not be accurately anchored. But Tom had it under very good control, and soon it was being held down on the ground by some of his helpers.

As all the sand ballast had been allowed to run out Tom was obliged to open the gas-valves and let some of the lifting vapor escape, or he could not have descended.

"Come on, now!" cried the inventor, as he leaped from the deck of his sky craft. "Let's clean out the red shed. That fire is only smothered, and there may be sparks smoldering under that sand, which will burst into flame, if we're not careful. Let's get the explosives out of the way."

"Bless my insurance policy, yes," exclaimed Mr. Damon. "That was a fine move of yours."

"It was the only way I could think of to put out the fire," Tom replied. "I knew water was out of the question, and sand was the next thing."

"But I didn't know where to get any until I happened to think of the ballast bags of my dirigible. Then I knew, if I could get above the fire, I could do the trick. I had to fly pretty high, though, as the fire was hot, and I was afraid it might explode the gas bag and wreck me."

"You were taking a chance," remarked Ned.

"Oh, well, you have to take chances in this business," observed Tom, with a smile. "Now, then, let's finish this work."

The sand, falling from the ballast bags of the dirigible, had so effectually quenched the fire that it was soon cool enough to permit close approach. Koku, Tom and some of the men who best knew how to handle the explosives, were soon engaged in the work of salvage.

"I wish I could help you, Tom," said his aged father. "I don't seem able to do anything but stand here and look on," and he gazed about him rather sadly.

"Never you mind, Dad!" Tom exclaimed. "We'll get along all right now. You'd better go up to the house. Mr. Damon will go with you."

"Yes, of course!" exclaimed the odd man, catching a wink from Tom, who wanted his father not to get too excited on account of his weak heart. "Come along, Professor Swift. The danger is all over."

"All right," assented the aged inventor, with a look at the still smoking shed.

"And, Dad, when you haven't anything else to do," went on Tom, rather whimsically, "you might be thinking up some plan to take up the recoil of those guns on my aerial warship. I confess I'm clean stumped on that point."

"Your aerial warship will never be a success," declared Mr. Swift. "You might as well give that up, Tom."

"Don't you believe it, Dad!" cried Tom, with more of a jolly air of one chum toward another than as though the talk was between father and son. "You solve the recoil problem for me, and I'll take care of the rest, and make the air warship sail. But we've got something else to do just now. Lively, boys."

While Mr. Swift, taking Mr. Damon's arm, walked toward the house, Tom, Ned, Koku, and some of the workmen began carrying out the explosives which had so narrowly escaped the fire. With long hooks the men pulled the shed apart, where the side walls had partly been burned through. Tom maintained an efficient firefighting force at his works, and the men had the proper tools with which to work.

Soon large openings were made on three sides of the red shed, or rather, what was left of it, and through these the dangerous chemicals and carbide, in sheet-iron cans, were carried out to a place of safety. In a little while nothing remained but a heap of hot sand, some charred embers and certain material that had been burned.

"Much loss, Tom?" asked Ned, as they surveyed the ruins. They were both black and grimy, tired and dirty, but there was a great sense of satisfaction.

"Well, yes, there's more lost than I like to think of," answered Tom slowly, "but it would have been a heap sight worse if the stuff had gone up. Still, I can replace what I've lost, except a few models I kept in this place. I really oughtn't to have stored them here, but since I've been working on my new aerial warship I have sort of let other matters slide. I intended to make the red shed nothing but a storehouse for explosive chemicals, but I still had some of my plans and models in it when it caught."

"Only for the sand the whole place might have gone," said Ned in a low voice.

"Yes. It's lucky I had plenty of ballast aboard the dirigible. You see, I've been running it alone lately, and I had to take on plenty of sand to make up for the weight of the several passengers I usually carry. So I had plenty of stuff to shower down on the fire. I wonder how it started, anyhow? I must investigate this."

"Mr. Damon and Eradicate seem to have seen it first," remarked Ned.

"Yes. At least they gave the alarm. Guess I'll ask Eradicate how he happened to notice. Oh, I say, Rad!" Tom called to the colored man.

"Yais, sah, Massa Tom! I'se comin'!" the darky cried, as he finished piling up, at a safe distance from the fire, a number of cans of carbide.

"How'd you happen to see the red shed ablaze?" Tom asked.

"Why, it was jest dish yeah way, Massa Tom," began the colored man. "I had jest been feedin' mah mule, Boomerang. He were pow'ful hungry, Boomerang were, an', when I give him some oats, wif a carrot sliced up in 'em—no, hole on—did I gib him a carrot t'day, or was it yist'day?—I done fo'got. No, it were yist'day I done gib him de carrot, I 'member now, 'case—"

"Oh, never mind the carrot, or Boomerang, either, Rad!" broke in Tom, "I'm asking you about the fire."

"An' I'se tellin' yo', Massa Tom," declared Eradicate, with a rather reproachful look at his master. "But I wanted t' do it right an' proper. I were comin' from Boomerang's stable, an' I see suffin' red spoutin' up at one corner ob de red shed. I knowed it were fire right away, an' I yelled."

"Yes, I heard you yell," Tom said. "But what I wanted to know is, did you see anyone near the red shed at the time?"

"No, Massa Tom, I done didn't."

"I wonder if Mr. Damon did? I must ask him," went on the young inventor. "Come, on, Ned, we'll go up to the house. Everything is all right here, I think. Whew! But that was some excitement. And I didn't show you my aerial warship after all! Nor have you settled that recoil problem for me."

"Time enough, I guess," responded Ned. "You sure did have a lucky escape, Tom."

"That's right. Well, Koku, what is it?" for the giant had approached, holding out something in his hand.

"Koku found this in red shed," went on the giant, holding out a round, blackened object. "Maybe him powder; go bang-bang!"

"Oh, you think it's something explosive, eh?" asked Tom, as he took the object from the giant.

"Koku no think much," was the answer. "Him look funny."

Tom did not speak for a moment. Then he cried:

"Look funny! I should say it did! See here, Ned, if this isn't suspicious I'll eat my hat!" and Tom beckoned excitedly to his chum, who had walked on a little in advance.

CHAPTER V
A QUEER STRANGER

What Tom Swift held in his hand looked like a small cannon ball, but it could not have been solid or the young aviator would not so easily have held it out at arm's length for his friend Ned Newton to look at.

"This puts a different face on it, Ned," Tom went on, as he turned the object over.

"Is that likely to go off?" the bank clerk asked, as he came to a halt a little distance from his friend.

"Go off? No, it's done all the damage it could, I guess."

"Damage? It looks to me as though it had suffered the most damage itself. What is it, one of your models? Looks like a bomb to me."

"And that's what it is, Ned."

"Not one of those you're going to use on your aerial warship, is it, Tom?"

"Not exactly. I never saw this before, but it's what started the fire in the red shed all right; I'm sure of that."

"Do you really mean it?" cried Ned.

"I sure do."

"Well, if that's the case, I wouldn't leave such dangerous things around where there are explosives, Tom."

"I didn't, Ned. I wouldn't have had this within a hundred miles of my shed, if I could have had my way. It's a fire bomb, and it was set to go off at a certain time. Only I think something went wrong, and the bomb started a fire ahead of time.

"If it had worked at night, when we were all asleep, we might not have put the fire out so easily. This sure is suspicious! I'm glad you found this, Koku."

Tom was carefully examining the bomb, as Ned had correctly named it. The bank clerk, now that he was assured by his chum that the object had done all the harm it could, approached closer.

What he saw was merely a hollow shell of iron, with a small opening in it, as though intended for a place through which to put a charge of explosives and a fuse.

"But there was no explosion, Tom," explained Ned.

"I know it," said Tom quietly. "It wasn't an explosive bomb. Smell that!"

He held the object under Ned's nose so suddenly that the young bank clerk jumped back.

"Oh, don't get nervous," laughed Tom. "It can't hurt you now. But what does that smell like?"

Ned sniffed, sniffed again, thought for a moment, and then sniffed a third time.

"Why," he said slowly, "I don't just know the name of it, but it's that funny stuff you mix up sometimes to put in the oxygen tanks when we go up in the rarefied atmosphere in the balloon or airship."

"Manganese and potash," spoke Tom. "That and two or three other things that form a chemical combination which goes off by itself of spontaneous combustion after a certain time. Only the person who put this bomb together didn't get the chemical mixture just right, and it went off ahead of time; for which we have to be duly thankful."

"Do you really think that, Tom?" cried Ned.

"I'm positive of it," was the quiet answer.

"Why—why—that would mean some one tried to set fire to the red shed, Tom!"

"They not only tried it, but did it," responded Tom, more coolly than seemed natural under the circumstances. "Only for the fact that the mixture went off before it was intended to, and found us all alert and ready—well, I don't like to think what might have happened," and Tom cast a look about at his group of buildings with their valuable contents.

"You mean some one purposely put that bomb in the red shed, Tom?"

"That's exactly what I mean. Some enemy, who wanted to do me an injury, planned this thing deliberately. He filled this steel shell with chemicals which, of themselves, after a certain time, would send out a hot tongue of flame through this hole," and Tom pointed to the opening in the round steel shell.

"He knew the fire would be practically unquenchable by ordinary means, and he counted on its soon eating its way into the carbide and other explosives. Only it didn't."

"Why, Tom!" cried Ned. "It was just like one of those alarm-clock dynamite bombs—set to go off at a certain time."

"Exactly," Tom said, "only this was more delicate, and, if it had worked properly, there wouldn't have been a vestige left to give us a clue. But the fire, thanks to the ballast sand in the dirigible, was put out in time. The fuse burned itself out, but I can tell by the smell that chemicals were in it. That's all, Koku," he went on to the giant who had stood waiting, not understanding all the talk between Tom and Ned. "I'll take care of this now."

"Bad man put it there?" asked the giant, who at least comprehended that something was wrong.

"Well, yes, I guess you could say it was a bad man," replied Tom.

"Ha! If Koku find bad man—bad for that man!" muttered the giant, as he clasped his two enormous hands together, as though they were already on the fellow who had tried to do Tom Swift such an injury.

"I wouldn't like to be that man, if Koku catches him," observed Ned. "Have you any idea who it could be, Tom?"

"Not the least. Of course I know I have enemies, Ned. Every successful inventor has persons who imagine he has stolen their ideas, whether he has ever seen them or not. It may have been one of those persons, or some half-mad crank, who was jealous. It would be impossible to say, Ned."

"It wouldn't be Andy Foger, would it?"

"No; I don't believe Andy has been in this neighborhood for some time. The last lesson we gave him sickened him, I guess."

"How about those diamond-makers, whose secret you discovered? They wouldn't be trying to get back at you, would they?"

"Well, it's possible, Ned. But I don't imagine so. They seem to have been pretty well broken up. No, I don't believe it was the diamond-makers who put this fire bomb in the red shed. Their line of activities didn't include this branch. It takes a chemist to know just how to blend the things contained in the bomb, and even a good chemist is likely to fail—as this one did, as far as time went."

"What are you going to do about it?" Ned asked.

"I don't know," and Tom spoke slowly, "I hoped I was done with all that sort of thing," he went on; "fighting enemies whom I have never knowingly injured. But it seems they are still after me. Well, Ned, this gives us something to do, at all events."

"You mean trying to find out who these fellows are?"

"Yes; that is, if you are willing to help."

"Well, I guess I am!" cried the bank clerk with sparkling eyes. "I wouldn't ask anything better. We've been in things like this before, Tom, and we'll go in again—and win! I'll help you all I can. Now, let's see if we can pick up any other clues. This is like old times!" and Ned laughed, for he, like Tom, enjoyed a good "fight," and one in which the odds were against them.

"We sure will have our hands full," declared the young inventor. "Trying to solve the problem of carrying guns on an aerial warship, and finding out who set this fire."

"Then you're not going to give up your aerial warship idea?"

"No, indeed!" Tom cried. "What made you think that?"

"Well, the way your father spoke—"

"Oh, dear old dad!" exclaimed Tom affectionately. "I don't want to argue with him, but he's dead wrong!"

"Then you are going to make a go of it?"

"I sure am, Ned! All I have to solve is the recoil proposition, and, as soon as we get straightened out from this fire, we'll tackle that problem again—you and I. But I sure would like to know who put this in my red shed," and Tom looked in a puzzled manner at the empty fire bomb he still held.

Tom paused, on his way to the house, to put the bomb in one of his offices.

"No use letting dad know about this," he went on. "It would only be something else for him to worry about."

"That's right," agreed Ned.

By this time nearly all evidences of the fire, except for the blackened ruins of the shed, had been cleared away. High in the air hung a cloud of black smoke, caused by some chemicals that had burned harmlessly save for that pall. Tom Swift had indeed had a lucky escape.

The young inventor, finding his father quieted down and conversing easily with Mr. Damon, who was blessing everything he could think of, motioned to Ned to follow him out of the house again.

"We'll leave dad here," said Tom, "and do a little investigating on our own account. We'll look for clues while they're fresh."

But, it must be confessed, after Tom and Ned had spent the rest of that day in and about the burned shed, they were little wiser than when they started. They found the place where the fire bomb had evidently been placed, right inside the main entrance to the shed. Tom knew it had been there because there were peculiar marks on the charred wood, and a certain queer smell of chemicals that confirmed his belief.

"They put the bomb there to prevent anyone going in at the first alarm and saving anything," Tom said. "They didn't count on the roof burning through first, giving me a chance to use the sand. I made the roof of the red shed flimsy just on that account, so the force of the explosion if one ever came, would be mostly upward. You know the expanding gases, caused by an explosion or by rapid combustion, always do just as electricity does, seek the shortest and easiest route. In this case I made the roof the easiest route."

"A lucky provision," observed Ned.

That night Tom had to confess himself beaten, as far as finding clues was concerned. The empty fire bomb was the only one, and that seemed valueless.

Close questioning of the workmen failed to disclose anything. Tom was particularly anxious to discover if any mysterious strangers had been seen about the works. There was a strict rule about admitting them to the plant, however, and it could not be learned that this had been violated.

"Well, we'll just have to lay that aside for a while," Tom said the next day, when Ned again came to pay a visit. "Now, what do you say to tackling, with me, that recoil problem on the aerial warship?"

"I'm ready, if you are," Ned agreed, "though I know about as much of those things as a snake does about dancing. But I'm game."

The two friends walked out toward the shed where Tom's new craft was housed. As yet Ned had not seen it. On the way they saw Eradicate walking along, talking to himself, as he often did.

"I wonder what he has on his mind," remarked Ned musingly.

"Something does seem to be worrying him," agreed Tom.

As they neared the colored man, they could hear him saying:

"He suah did hab nerve, dat's what he did! De idea ob askin' me all dem questions, an' den wantin' t' know if I'd sell him!"

"What's that, Eradicate?" asked Tom.

"Oh, it's a man I met when I were comin' back from de ash dump," Eradicate explained. One of the colored man's duties was to cart ashes away from Tom's various shops, and dump them in a certain swampy lot. With an old ramshackle cart, and his mule, Boomerang, Eradicate did this task to perfection.

"A man—what sort of a man?" asked Tom, always ready to be suspicious of anything unusual.

"He were a queer man," went on the aged colored helper. "First he stopped me an' asted me fo' a ride. He was a dressed-up gen'man, too, an' I were suah s'prised at him wantin' t' set in mah ole ash cart," said Eradicate. "But I done was polite t' him, an' fixed a blanket so's he wouldn't git too dirty. Den he asted me ef I didn't wuk fo' yo', Massa Tom, an' of course I says as how I did. Den he asted me about de fire, an' how much damage it done, an' how we put it out. An' he end up by sayin' he'd laik t' buy mah mule, Boomerang, an' he wants t' come heah dis arternoon an' talk t' me about it."

"He does, eh?" cried Tom. "What sort of a man was he, Rad?"

"Well, a gen'man sort ob man, Massa Tom. Stranger t' me. I nebber seed him afo'. He suah was monstrous polite t' ole black Eradicate, an' he gib me a half-dollar, too, jest fo' a little ride. But I aint' gwine t' sell Boomerang, no indeedy, I ain't!" and Eradicate shook his gray, kinky head decidedly.

"Ned, there may be something in this!" said Tom, in an excited whisper to his chum. "I don't like the idea of a mysterious stranger questioning Eradicate!"

CHAPTER VI
THE AERIAL WARSHIP

Ned Newton looked at Tom questioningly. Then he glanced at the unsuspicious colored man, who was industriously polishing the half-dollar the mysterious stranger had given him.

"Rad, just exactly what sort of a man was this one you speak of?" asked Tom.

"Why, he were a gen'man—"

"Yes, I know that much. You've said it before. But was he an Englishman, an American—or—"

Tom paused and waited for an answer.

"I think he were a Frenchman," spoke Eradicate. "I done didn't see him eat no frogs' laigs, but he smoked a cigarette dat had a funny smell, and he suah was monstrous polite. He suah was a Frenchman. I think."

Tom and Ned laughed at Eradicate's description of the man, but Tom's face was soon grave again.

"Tell us more about him, Rad," he suggested. "Did he seem especially interested in the fire?"

"No, sah, Massa Tom, he seemed laik he was more special interested in mah mule, Boomerang. He done asted how long I had him, an' how much I wanted fo' him, an' how old he was."

"But every once in a while he put in some question about the fire, or about our shops, didn't he, Rad?" Tom wanted to know.

The colored man scratched his kinky head, and glanced with a queer look at Tom.

"How yo' all done guess dat?" he asked.

"Answer my question," insisted Tom.

"Yes, sah, he done did ask about yo', and de wuks, ebery now and den," Rad confessed. "But how yo' all knowed dat, Massa Tom, when I were a-tellin' yo' all about him astin' fo' mah mule, done gets me—dat's what it suah does."

"Never mind, Rad. He asked questions about the plant, that's all I want to know. But you didn't tell him much, did you?"

Eradicate looked reproachfully at his master.

"Yo' all done knows me bettah dan dat, Massa Tom," the old colored man said. "Yo' all know yo' done gib orders fo' nobody t' talk about yo' projections."

"Yes, I know I gave those orders," Tom said, with a smile, "but I want to make sure that they have been followed."

"Well, I done follered 'em, Massa Tom."

"Then you didn't tell this queer stranger, Frenchman, or whatever he is, much about my place?"

"I didn't tell him nuffin', sah. I done frowed dust in his eyes."

Ned uttered an exclamation of surprise.

"Eradicate is speaking figuratively," Tom said, with a laugh.

"Dat's what I means," the colored man went on. "I done fooled him. When he asted me about de fire I said it didn't do no damage at all—in fack dat we'd rather hab de fire dan not hab it, 'case it done gib us a chance t' practice our hose drill."

"That's good," laughed Tom. "What else?"

"Well, he done sort ob hinted t' me ef we all knowed how de fire done start. I says as how we did, dat we done start it ourse'ves fo' practice, an dat we done expected it all along, an' were ready fo' it. Course I knows dat were a sort of fairy story, Massa Tom, but den dat cigarette-smokin' Frenchman didn't hab no right t' asted me so many questions, did he?"

"No, indeed, Rad. And I'm glad you didn't give him straight answers. So he's coming here later on, is he?"

"T' see ef I wants t' sell mah mule, Boomerang, yais, sah. I sort ob thought maybe you'd want t' hab a look at dat man, so I tole him t' come on. Course I doan' want t' sell Boomerang, but ef he was t' offer me a big lot ob money fo' him I'd take it."

"Of course," Tom answered. "Very well, Rad. You may go on now, and don't say anything to anyone about what you have told me."

"I won't, Massa Tom," promised the colored man, as he went off muttering to himself.

"Well, what do you make of it, Tom?" asked Ned of his chum, as they walked on toward the shed of the new, big aerial warship.

"I don't know just what to think, Ned. Of course things like this have happened before—persons trying to worm secrets out of Eradicate, or some of the other men."

"They never succeeded in getting much, I'm glad to say, but it always keeps me worried for fear something will happen," Tom concluded.

"But about this Frenchman?"

"Well, he must be a new one. And, now I come to think of it, I did hear some of the men speaking about a foreigner—a stranger—being around town last week. It was just a casual reference, and I paid little attention to it. Now it looks as though there might be something in it."

"Do you think he'll come to bargain with Eradicate about the mule?" Ned asked.

"Hardly. That was only talk to make Eradicate unsuspicious. The stranger, whoever he was, sized Rad up partly right. I surmised, when Rad said he asked a lot of questions about the mule, that was only to divert suspicion, and that he'd come back to the subject of the fire every chance he got."

"And you were right."

"Yes, so it seems. But I don't believe the fellow will come around here. It would be too risky. All the same, we'll be prepared for him. I'll just rig up one of my photo-telephone machines, so that, if he does come to have a talk with Rad, we can both see and hear him."

"That's great, Tom! But do you think this fellow had anything to do with the fire?"

"I don't know. He knew about it, of course. This isn't the first fire we've had in the works, and, though we always fight them ourselves, still news of it will leak out to the town. So he could easily have known about it. And he might be in with those who set it, for I firmly believe the fire was set by someone who has an object in injuring me."

"It's too bad!" declared Ned. "Seems as though they might let you alone, if they haven't gumption enough to invent things for themselves."

"Well, don't worry. Maybe it will come out all right," returned Tom. "Now, let's go and have a look at my aerial warship. I haven't shown it to you yet. Then we'll get ready for that mysterious Frenchman, if he comes—but I don't believe he will."

The young inventor unlocked the door of the shed where he kept his latest "pet," and at the sight which met his eyes Ned Newton uttered an exclamation of surprise.

"Tom, what is it?" he cried in an awed voice.

"My aerial warship!" was the quiet answer.

Ned Newton gave vent to a long whistle, and then began a detailed examination of the wonderful craft he saw before him. That is, he made as detailed an examination as was possible under the circumstances, for it was a long time before the young bank clerk fully appreciated all Tom Swift had accomplished in building the Mars, which was the warlike name painted in red letters on the big gas container that tugged and swayed overhead.

"Tom, however did you do it?" gasped Ned at length.

"By hard work," was the modest reply. "I've been at this for a longer time than you'd suppose, working on it at odd moments. I had a lot of help, too, or I never could have done it. And now it is nearly all finished, as far as the ship itself is concerned. The only thing that bothers me is to provide for the recoil of the guns I want to carry. Maybe you can help me with that. Come on, now, I'll explain how the affair works, and what I hope to accomplish with it."

In brief Tom's aerial warship was a sort of German Zeppelin type of dirigible balloon, rising in the air by means of a gas container, or, rather, several of them, for the section for holding the lifting gas element was divided by bulkheads.

The chief difference between dirigible balloons and ordinary aeroplanes, as you all know, is that the former are lifted from the earth by a gas, such as hydrogen, which is lighter than air, while the aeroplane lifts itself by getting into motion, when broad, flat planes, or surfaces, hold it up, just as a flat stone is held up when you sail it through the air. The moment the stone, or aeroplane, loses its forward motion, it begins to fall.

This is not so with a dirigible balloon. It is held in the air by means of the lifting gas, and once so in the air can be sent in any direction by means of propellers and rudders.

Tom's aerial warship contained many new features. While it was as large as some of the war-type Zeppelins, it differed from them materially. But the details would be of more interest to a scientific builder of such things than to the ordinary reader, so I will not weary you with them.

Sufficient to say that Tom's craft consisted first of a great semi-rigid bag, or envelope, made of specially prepared oiled silk and aluminum, to hold the gas, which was manufactured on board. There were a number of gas-tight compartments, so that if one, or even if a number of them burst, or were shot by an enemy, the craft would still remain afloat.

Below the big gas bag was the ship proper, a light but strong and rigid framework about which were built enclosed cabins. These cabins, or compartments, housed the driving machinery, the gas-generating plant, living, sleeping and dining quarters, and a pilot-house, whence the ship could be controlled.

But this was not all.

Ned, making a tour of the Mars, as she swayed gently in the big shed, saw where several aluminum pedestals were mounted, fore and aft and on either beam of the ship.

"They look just like places where you intend to mount guns," said Ned to Tom.

"And that's exactly what they are," the young inventor replied. "I have the guns nearly ready for mounting, but I can't seem to think of a way of providing for the recoil. And if I don't take care of that, I'm likely to find my ship coming apart under me, after we bombard the enemy with a broadside or two."

"Then you intend to fight with this ship?" asked Ned.

"Well, no; not exactly personally. I was thinking of offering it to the United States Government. Foreign nations are getting ready large fleets of aerial warships, so why shouldn't we? Matters in Europe are mighty uncertain. There may be a great war there in which aerial craft will play a big part. I am conceited enough to think I can build one that will measure up to the foreign ones, and I'll soon be in a position to know."

"What do you mean?"

"I mean I have already communicated with our government experts, and they are soon to come and inspect this craft. I have sent them word that it is about finished. There is only the matter of the guns, and some of the ordnance officers may be able to help me out with a suggestion, for I admit I am stuck!" exclaimed Tom.

"Then you're going to do the same with this aerial warship as you did with your big lantern and that immense gun you perfected?" asked Ned.

"That's right," confirmed Tom. My former readers will know to what Ned Newton referred, and those of you who do not may learn the details of how Tom helped Uncle Sam, by reading the previous volumes, "Tom Swift and His Great Searchlight," and "Tom Swift and His Giant Cannon."

"When do you expect the government experts?" Ned asked.

"Within a few days, now. But I'll have to hustle to get ready for them, as this fire has put me back. There are quite a number of details I need to change. Well, now, let me explain about that gun recoil business. Maybe you can help me."

"Fire away," laughed Ned. "I'll do the best I can."

Tom led the way from the main shed, where the aerial warship was housed, to a small private office. As Ned entered, the door, pulled by a strong spring, swung after him. He held back his hand to prevent it from slamming, but there was no need, for a patent arrangement took up all the force, and the door closed gently. Ned looked around, not much surprised, for the same sort of door-check was in use at his bank. But a sudden idea came to him.

"There you are, Tom!" he cried. "Why not take up the recoil of the guns on your aerial warship by some such device as that?" and Ned pointed to the door-check.

CHAPTER VII
WARNINGS

For a moment or two Tom Swift did not seem to comprehend what Ned had said. He remained staring, first at his chum, who stood pointing, and from him Tom's gaze wandered to the top of the door. It may have been, and probably was, that Tom was thinking of other matters at that instant. But Ned said again:

"Wouldn't that do, Tom? Check the recoil of the gun with whatever stuff is in that arrangement!"

A sudden change came over Tom's face. It was lighted up with a gleam of understanding.

"By Jove, Ned, old man!" he cried. "I believe you've struck it! And to think that has been under my nose, or, rather, over my head, all this while, and I never thought of it. Hurray! That will solve the problem!"

"Do you think it will?" asked Ned, glad that he had contributed something, if only an idea, to Tom's aerial warship.

"I'm almost sure it will. I'll give it a trial right away."

"What's in that door-check?" Ned asked. "I never stopped before to think what useful things they are, though at the bank, with the big, heavy doors, they are mighty useful."

"They are a combination of springs and hydrostatic valves," began Tom.

"Good-night!" laughed Ned. "Excuse the slang, Tom, but what in the world is a hydrostatic valve?"

"A valve through which liquids pass. In this door-check there may be a mixture of water, alcohol and glycerine, the alcohol to prevent freezing in cold weather, and the glycerine to give body to the mixture so it will not flow through the valves too freely."

"And do you think you can put something like that on your guns, so the recoil will be taken up?" Ned wanted to know.

"I think so," spoke Tom. "I'm going to work on it right away, and we'll soon see how it will turn out. It's mighty lucky you thought of that, for I sure was up against it, as the boys say."

"It just seemed to come to me," spoke Ned, "seeing how easily the door closed."

"If the thing works I'll give you due credit for it," promised Tom. "Now, I've got to figure out how much force a modified hydrostatic valve check like that will take up, and how much recoil my biggest gun will have."

"Then you're going to put several guns on the Mars?" asked Ned.

"Yes, four quick-firers, at least, two on each side, and heavier guns at the bow and stern, to throw explosive shells in a horizontal or upward direction. For a downward direction we won't need any guns, we can simply drop the bombs, or shells, from a release clutch."

"Drop them on other air craft?" Ned wanted to know.

"Well, if it's necessary, yes. Though I guess there won't be much chance of doing that to a rival aeroplane or dirigible. But in flying over cities or forts, explosive bombs can be dropped very nicely. For use in attacking other air craft I am going to depend on my lateral fire, from the guns mounted on either beam, and in the bow and stern."

"You speak as though you, yourself, were going into a battle of the air," said Ned.

"No, I don't believe I'll go that far," Tom replied. "Though, if the government wants my craft, I may have to go aloft and fire shots at targets for them to show them how things work.

"Please don't think that I am in favor of war, Ned," went on Tom earnestly. "I hate it, and I wish the time would come when all nations would disarm. But if the other countries are laying themselves out to have aerial battleships, it is time the United States did also. We must not be left behind, especially in view of what is taking place in Europe."

"I suppose that's right," agreed Ned. "Have you any of your guns ready?"

"Yes, all but the mounting of them on the supports aboard the Mars. I haven't dared do that yet, and fire them, until I provided some means of taking up the recoil. Now I'm going to get right to work on that problem."

There was considerable detailed figuring and computation work ahead of Tom Swift, and I will not weary you by going into the details of higher mathematics. Even Ned lost interest after the start of the problem, though he was interested when Tom took down the door-check and began measuring the amount of force it would take up, computing it on scales and spring balances.

Once this had been done, and Tom had figured just how much force could be expected to be taken up by a larger check, with stronger hydrostatic valves, the young inventor explained:

"And now to see how much recoil force my guns develop!"

"Are you really going to fire the guns?" asked Ned.

"Surely," answered Tom. "That's the only way to get at real results. I'll have the guns taken out and mounted in a big field. Then we'll fire them, and measure the recoil."

"Well, that may be some fun," spoke Ned, with a grin. "More fun than all these figures," and he looked at the mass of details on Tom's desk.

This was the second or third day after the fire in the red shed, and in the interim Tom had been busy making computations. These were about finished. Meanwhile further investigation had been made of clues leading to the origin of the blaze in the shed, but nothing had been learned.

A photo-telephone had been installed near Eradicate's quarters, in the hope that the mysterious stranger might keep his promise, and come to see about the mule. In that case something would have been learned about him. But, as Tom feared, the man did not appear.

Ned was much interested in the guns, and, a little later, he helped Tom and Koku mount them in a vacant lot. The giant's strength came in handy in handling the big parts.

Mr. Swift strolled past, as the guns were being mounted for the preliminary test, and inquired what his son was doing.

"It will never work, Tom, never!" declared the aged inventor, when informed. "You can't take up those guns in your air craft, and fire them with any degree of safety."

"You wait, Dad," laughed Tom. "You haven't yet seen how the Newton hydrostatic recoil operates."

Ned smiled with pleasure at this.

It took nearly a week to get all the guns mounted, for some of them required considerable work, and it was also necessary to attach gauges to them to register the recoil and pressure. In the meanwhile Tom had been in further communication with government experts who were soon to call on him to inspect the aerial warship, with a view to purchase.

"When are they coming?" asked Ned, as he and Tom went out one morning to make the first test of the guns.

"They will be here any day, now. They didn't set any definite date. I suppose they want to take us unawares, to see that I don't 'frame-up' any game on them. Well, I'll be ready any time they come. Now, Koku, bring along those shells, and don't drop any of them, for that new powder is freakish stuff."

"Me no drop any, Master," spoke the giant, as he lifted the boxes of explosives in his strong arms.

The largest gun was loaded and aimed at a distant hill, for Tom knew that if the recoil apparatus would take care of the excess force of his largest gun, the problem of the smaller ones would be easy to solve.

"Here, Rad, where are you going?" Tom asked, as he noticed the colored man walking away, after having completed a task assigned to him.

"Where's I gwine, Massa Tom?"

"Yes, Rad, that's what I asked you."

"I—I'se gwine t' feed mah mule, Boomerang," said the colored man slowly. "It's his eatin' time, jest now, Massa Tom."

"Nonsense! It isn't anywhere near noon yet."

"Yais, sab, Massa Tom, I knows dat," said Eradicate, as he carefully edged away from the big gun, "but I'se done changed de eatin' hours ob dat mule. He had a little touch ob indigestion de udder day, an' I'se feedin' him diff'rent now. So I guess as how yo'll hab t' 'scuse me now, Massa Tom."

"Oh, well, trot along," laughed the young inventor. "I guess we won't need you. Is everything all right there, Koku?"

"All right, Master."

"Now, Ned, if you'll stand here," went on Tom, "and note the extreme point to which the hand on the pressure gauge goes, I'll be obliged to you. Just jot it down on this pad."

"Here comes someone," remarked the bank clerk, as he saw that his pencil was sharpened. He pointed to the field back of them.

"It's Mr. Damon," observed Tom. "We'll wait until he arrives. He'll be interested in this."

"Bless my collar button, Tom! What's going on?" asked the eccentric man, as he came up. "Has war been declared?"

"Just practicing," replied the young inventor. "Getting ready to put the armament on my aerial warship."

"Well, as long as I'm behind the guns I'm all right, I suppose?"

"Perfectly," Tom replied. "Now then, Ned, I think we'll fire."

There was a moment of inspection, to see that nothing had been forgotten, and then the big gun was discharged. There was a loud report, not as heavy, though, as Ned had expected, but there was no puff of smoke, for Tom was using smokeless powder. Only a little flash of flame was observed.

"Catch the figure, Ned!" Tom cried.

"I have it!" was the answer. "Eighty thousand!"

"Good! And I can build a recoil check that will take up to one hundred and twenty thousand pounds pressure. That ought to be margin of safety enough. Now we'll try another shot."

The echoes of the first had hardly died away before the second gun was ready for the test. That, too, was satisfactory, and then the smaller ones were operated. These were not quite so satisfactory, as the recoil developed was larger, in proportion to their size, than Tom had figured.

"But I can easily put a larger hydrostatic check on them," he said. "Now, we'll fire by batteries, and see what the total is."

Then began a perfect bombardment of the distant hillside, service charges being used, and explosive shells sent out so that dirt, stones and gravel flew in all directions. Danger signs and flags had been posted, and a cordon of Tom's men kept spectators away from the hill, so no one would be in the danger zone.

The young inventor was busy making some calculations after the last of the firing had been completed. Koku was packing up the unfired shells, and Mr. Damon was blessing his ear-drums, and the pieces of cotton he had stuffed in to protect them, when a tall, erect man was observed strolling over the fields in the direction of the guns.

"Somebody's coming, Tom," warned Ned.

"Yes, and a stranger, too," observed Tom. "I wonder if that can be Eradicate's Frenchman?"

But a look at the stranger's face disproved that surmise. He had a frank and pleasant countenance, obviously American.

"I beg your pardon," he began, addressing everyone in general, "but I am looking for Tom Swift. I was told he was here."

"I am Tom Swift," replied our hero.

"Ah! Well, I am Lieutenant Marbury, with whom you had some correspondence recently about—"

"Oh, yes, Lieutenant Marbury, of the United States Navy," interrupted Tom. "I'm glad to see you," he went on, holding out his hand. "We are just completing some tests with the guns. You called, I presume, in reference to my aerial warship?"

"That is it—yes. Have you it ready for a trial flight?"

"Well, almost. It can be made ready in a few hours. You see, I have been delayed. There was a fire in the plant."

"A fire!" exclaimed the officer in surprise. "How was that? We heard nothing of it in Washington."

"No, I kept it rather quiet," Tom explained. "We had reason to suspect that it was a fire purposely set, in a shed where I kept a quantity of explosives."

"Ha!" exclaimed Lieutenant Marbury. "This fits in with what I have heard. And did you not receive warning?" he asked Tom.

"Warning? No. Of what?"

"Of foreign spies!" was the unexpected answer. "I am sorry. Some of our Secret Service men unearthed something of a plot against you, and I presumed you had been told to watch out. If you had, the fire might not have occurred. There must have been some error in Washington. But let me tell you now, Tom Swift—be on your guard!"

CHAPTER VIII
A SUSPECTED PLOT

The officer's words were so filled with meaning that Tom started. Ned Newton, too, showed the effect he felt.

"Do you really mean that?" asked the young inventor, looking around to make sure his father was not present. On account of Professor Swift's weak heart, Tom wished to spare him all possible worry.

"I certainly do mean it," insisted Lieutenant Marbury. "And, while I am rather amazed at the news of the fire, for I did not think the plotters would be so bold as that, it is in line with what I expected, and what we suspected in Washington."

"And that was—what?" asked Tom.

"The existence of a well-laid plot, not only against our government, but against you!"

"And why have they singled me out?" Tom demanded.

"I might as well tell it from the beginning," the officer went on. "As long as you have not received any official warning from Washington you had better hear the whole story. But are you sure you had no word?"

"Well, now, I won't be so sure," Tom confessed. "I have been working very hard, the last two days, making some intricate calculations. I have rather neglected my mail, to tell you the truth.

"And, come to think of it, there were several letters received with the Washington postmark. But, I supposed they had to do with some of my patents, and I only casually glanced over them. There was one letter, though, that I couldn't make head or tail of."

"Ha! That was it!" cried the lieutenant. "It was the warning in cipher or code. I didn't think they would neglect to send it to you."

"But what good would it do me if I couldn't read it?" asked Tom.

"You must also have received a method of deciphering the message," the officer said. "Probably you overlooked that. The Secret Service men sent you the warning in code, so it would not be found out by the plotters, and, to make sure you could understand it, a method of translating the cipher was sent in a separate envelope. It is too bad you missed it."

"Yes, for I might have been on my guard," agreed Tom. "The red shed might not have burned, but, as it was, only slight damage was done."

"Owing to the fact that Tom put the fire out with sand ballast from his dirigible!" cried Ned. "You should have seen it!"

"I should have liked to be here," the lieutenant spoke. "But, if I were you, Tom Swift, I would take means to prevent a repetition of such things."

"I shall," Tom decided. "But, if we want to talk, we had better go to my office, where we can be more private. I don't want the workmen to hear too much."

Now that the firing was over, a number of Tom's men from the shops had assembled around the cannon. Most of them, the young inventor felt, could be trusted, but in so large a gathering one could never be sure.

"Did you come on from Washington yesterday?" asked Tom, as he, Ned and the officer strolled toward the shed where was housed the aerial warship.

"Yes, and I spent the night in New York. I arrived in town a short time ago, and came right on out here. At your house I was told you were over in the fields conducting experiments, so I came on here."

"Glad you did," Tom said. "I'll soon have something to show you, I hope. But I am interested in hearing the details of this suspected plot. Are you sure one exists?"

"Perfectly sure," was the answer. "We don't know all the details yet, nor who are concerned in it, but we are working on the case. The Secret Service has several agents in the field.

"We are convinced in Washington," went on Lieutenant Marbury, when he, Tom and Ned were seated in the private office, "that foreign spies are at work against you and against our government."

"Why against me?" asked Tom, in wonder.

"Because of the inventions you have perfected and turned over to Uncle Sam—notably the giant cannon, which rivals anything foreign European powers have, and the great searchlight, which proved so effective against the border smugglers. The success of those two alone, to say nothing of your submarine, has not only made foreign nations jealous, but they fear you—and us," the officer went on.

"Well, if they only take it out in fear—"

"But they won't!" interrupted the officer—"They are seeking to destroy those inventions. More than once, of late, we have nipped a plot just in time."

"Have they really tried to damage the big gun?" asked Tom, referring to one he had built and set up at Panama.

"They have. And now this fire proves that they are taking other measures—they are working directly against you."

"Why, I wonder?"

"Either to prevent you from making further inventions, or to stop you from completing your latest—the aerial warship."

"But I didn't know the foreign governments knew about that," Tom exclaimed. "It was a secret."

"Few secrets are safe from foreign Spies," declared Lieutenant Marbury. "They have a great ferreting-out system on the other side. We are just beginning to appreciate it. But our own men have not been idle."

"Have they really learned anything?" Tom asked. "Nothing definite enough to warrant us in acting," was the answer of the government man. "But we know enough to let us see that the plot is far-reaching."

"Are the French in it?" asked Ned impulsively.

"The French! Why do you ask that?"

"Tell him about Eradicate, and the man who wanted to buy the mule, Tom," suggested Ned.

Thereupon the young inventor mentioned the story told by Eradicate. He also brought out the fire-bomb, and explained his theory as to how it had operated to set the red shed ablaze.

"I think you are right," said Lieutenant Marbury. "And, as regards the French, I might say they are not the only nation banded to obtain our secrets—yours and the government's!"

"But I thought the French and the English were friendly toward us!" Ned exclaimed.

"So they are, in a certain measure," the officer went on. "And Russia is, too. But, in all foreign countries there are two parties, the war party, as it might be called, and the peace element.

"But I might add that it is neither France, England, nor Russia that we must fear. It is a certain other great nation, which at present I will not name."

"And you think spies set this fire?"

"I certainly do."

"But what measures shall I adopt against this plot?" Tom asked.

"We will talk that over," said Lieutenant Marbury. "But, before I go into details, I want to give you another warning. You must be very careful about—"

A sudden knock on the door interrupted the speaker.

CHAPTER IX
THE RECOIL CHECK

"Who is that?" asked Ned Newton, with a quick glance at his chum.

"I don't know," Tom answered. "I left orders we weren't to be disturbed unless it was something important."

"May be something has happened," suggested the navy officer, "another fire, perhaps, or a—"

"It isn't a fire," Tom answered. "The automatic alarm would be ringing before this in that case."

The knock was repeated. Tom went softly to the door and opened it quickly, to disclose, standing in the corridor, one of the messengers employed about the shops.

"Well, what is it?" asked Tom a bit sharply.

"Oh, if you please, Mr. Swift," said the boy, "a man has applied for work at the main office, and you know you left orders there that if any machinists came along, we were to—"

"Oh, so I did," Tom exclaimed. "I had forgotten about that," he went on to Lieutenant Marbury and Ned. "I am in need of helpers to rush through the finishing touches on my aerial warship, and I left word, if any applied, as they often do, coming here from other cities, that I wanted to see them. How many are there?" Tom asked of the messenger.

"Two, this time. They both say they're good mechanics."

"That's what they all say," interposed Tom, with a smile. "But, though they may be good mechanics in their own line, they need to have special qualifications to work on airships. Tell them to wait, Rodney," Tom went on to the lad, "and I'll see them presently."

As the boy went away, and Tom closed the door, he turned to Lieutenant Marbury.

"You were about to give me another warning when that interruption came. You might complete it now."

"Yes, it was another warning," spoke the officer, "and one I hope you will heed. It concerns yourself, personally."

"Do you mean he is in danger?" asked Ned quickly.

"That's exactly what I do mean," was the prompt reply. "In danger of personal injury, if not something worse."

Tom did not seem as alarmed as he might reasonably have been under the circumstances.

"Danger, eh?" he repeated coolly. "On the part of whom?"

"That's just where I can't warn you," the officer replied. "I can only give you that hint, and beg of you to be careful."

"Do you mean you are not allowed to tell?" asked Ned.

"No, indeed; it isn't that!" the lieutenant hastened to assure the young man. "I would gladly tell, if I knew. But this plot, like the other one, directed against the inventions themselves, is so shrouded in mystery that I cannot get to the bottom of it.

"Our Secret Service men have been working on it for some time, not only in order to protect you, because of what you have done for the government, but because Uncle Sam wishes to protect his own property, especially the searchlight and the big cannon. But, though our agents have worked hard, they have not been able to get any clues that would put them on the right trail.

"So we can only warn you to be careful, and this I do in all earnestness. That was part of my errand in coming here, though, of course, I am anxious to inspect the new aerial warship you have constructed. So watch out for two things—your inventions, and, more than all, your life!"

"Do you really think they would do me bodily harm?" Tom asked, a trifle skeptical.

"I certainly do. These foreign spies are desperate. If they cannot secure the use of these inventions to their own country, they are determined not to let this country have the benefit of them."

"Well, I'll be careful," Tom promised. "I'm no more anxious than anyone else to run my head into danger, and I certainly don't want any of my shops or inventions destroyed. The fire in the red shed was as close as I want anything to come."

"That's right!" agreed Ned. "And, if there's anything I can do, Tom, don't hesitate to call on me."

"All right, old man. I won't forget. And now, perhaps, you would like to see the Mars," he said to the lieutenant.

"I certainly would," was the ready answer. "But hadn't you better see those men who are waiting to find out about positions here?"

"There's no hurry about them," Tom said. "We have applicants every day, and it's earlier than the hour when I usually see them. They can wait. Now I want your opinion on my new craft. But, you must remember that it is not yet completed, and only recently did I begin to solve the problem of mounting the guns. So be a little easy with your criticisms."

Followed by Ned and Lieutenant Marbury, Tom led the way into the big airship shed. There, swaying about at its moorings, was the immense aerial warship. To Ned's eyes it looked complete enough, but, when Tom pointed out the various parts, and explained to the government officer how it was going to work, Ned understood that considerable yet remained to be done on it.

Tom showed his official guest how a new system of elevation and depressing rudders had been adopted, how a new type of propeller was to be used and indicated several other improvements. The lower, or cabin, part of the aircraft could be entered by mounting a short ladder from the ground, and Tom took Ned and Lieutenant Marbury through the engine-room and other compartments of the Mars.

"It certainly is most complete," the officer observed. "And when you get the guns mounted I shall be glad to make an official test. You understand," he went on, to Tom, "that we are vitally interested in the guns, since we now have many aircraft that can be used purely for scouting purposes. What we want is something for offense, a veritable naval terror of the seas."

"I understand," Tom answered. "And I am going to begin work on mounting the guns at once. I am going to use the Newton recoil check," he added. "Ned, here, is responsible for that."

"Is that so?" asked the lieutenant, as Tom clapped his chum on the back.

"Yes, that's his invention."

"Oh, it isn't anything of the sort," Ned objected. "I just—"

"Yes, he just happened to solve the problem for me!" interrupted Tom, as he told the story of the door-spring.

"A good idea!" commented Lieutenant Marbury.

Tom then briefly described the principle on which his aerial warship would work, explaining how the lifting gas would raise it, with its load of crew, guns and explosives, high into the air; how it could then be sent ahead, backward, to either side, or around in a circle, by means of the propellers and the rudders, and how it could be raised or lowered, either by rudders or by forcing more gas into the lifting bags, or by letting some of the vapor out.

And, while this was being done by the pilot or captain in charge, the crew could be manning the guns with which hostile airships would be attacked, and bombs dropped on the forts or battleships of the enemy.

"It seems very complete," observed the lieutenant. "I shall be glad when I can give it an official test."

"Which ought to be in about a week," Tom said. "Meanwhile I shall be glad if you will be my guest here."

And so that was arranged.

Leaving Ned and the lieutenant to entertain each other, Tom went to see the mechanics who had applied for places. He found them satisfactory and engaged them. One of them had worked for him before. The other was a stranger, but he had been employed in a large aeroplane factory, and brought good recommendations.

There followed busy days at the Swift plant, and work was pushed on the aerial warship. The hardest task was the mounting of the guns, and equipping them with the recoil check, without which it would be impossible to fire them with the craft sailing through the air.

But finally one of the big guns, and two of the smaller ones were in place, with the apparatus designed to reduce the recoil shock, and then Tom decided to have a test of the Mars.

"Up in the air, do you mean?" asked Ned, who was spending all his spare time with his chum.

"Well, a little way up in the air, at least," Tom answered. "I'll make a sort of captive balloon of my craft, and see how she behaves. I don't want to take too many chances with that new recoil check, though it seems to work perfectly in theory."

The day came when, for the first time, the Mars was to come out of the big shed where she had been constructed. The craft was not completed for a flight as yet, but could be made so in a few days, with rush work. The roof of the great shed slid back, and the big envelope containing the buoyant gas rose slowly upward. There was a cry of surprise from the many workmen in the yard, as they saw, most of them for the first time, the wonderful new craft. It did not go up very high, being held in place with anchor ropes.

The sun glistened on the bright brass and nickel parts, and glinted from the gleaming barrels of the quick-firing guns.

"That's enough!" Tom called to the men below, who were paying out the ropes from the windlasses. "Hold her there."

Tom, Ned, Lieutenant Marbury and Mr. Damon were aboard the captive Mars.

Looking about, to see that all was in readiness, Tom gave orders to load the guns, blank charges being used, of course.

The recoil apparatus was in place, and it now remained to see if it would do the work for which it was designed.

"All ready?" asked the young inventor.

"Bless my accident insurance policy!" exclaimed Mr. Damon. "I'm as ready as ever I shall be, Tom. Let 'em go!"

"Hold fast!" cried Tom, as he prepared to press the electrical switch which would set off the guns. Ned and Lieutenant Marbury stood near the indicators to notice how much of the recoil would be neutralized by the check apparatus.

"Here we go!" cried the young inventor, and, at the same moment, from down below on the ground, came a warning cry:

"Don't shoot, Massa Tom. Don't shoot! Mah mule, Boomerang—"

But Eradicate had spoken too late. Tom pressed the switch; there was a deafening crash, a spurt of flame, and then followed wild cries and confused shouts, while the echoes of the reports rolled about the hills surrounding Shopton.

CHAPTER X
THE NEW MEN

"What was the matter down there?"

"Was anyone hurt?"

"Don't forget to look at those pressure gauges!"

"Bless my ham sandwich!"

Thus came the cries from those aboard the captive Mars. Ned, Lieutenant Marbury and Tom had called out in the order named. And, of course, I do not need to tell you what remark Mr. Damon made. Tom glanced toward where Ned and the government man stood, and saw that they had made notes of the pressure recorded on the recoil checks directly after the guns were fired. Mr. Damon, blessing innumerable objects under his breath, was looking over the side of the rail to discover the cause of the commotion and cries of warning from below.

"I don't believe it was anything serious, Tom," said the odd man. "No one seems to be hurt." "Look at Eradicate!" suddenly exclaimed Ned.

"And his mule! I guess that's what the trouble was, Tom!"

They looked to where the young bank employee pointed, and saw the old colored man, seated on the seat of his ramshackle wagon, doing his best to pull down to a walk the big galloping mule, which was dragging the vehicle around in a circle.

"Whoa, dere!" Eradicate was shouting, as he pulled on the lines. "Whoa, dere! Dat's jest laik yo', Boomerang, t' run when dere ain't no call fo' it, nohow! Ef I done wanted yo' t' git a move on, yo'd lay down 'side de road an' go to sleep. Whoa, now!"

But the noise of the shots had evidently frightened the long-eared animal, and he was in no mood for stopping, now that he had once started. It was not until some of the workmen ran out from the group where they had gathered to watch Tom's test, and got in front of Boomerang, that they succeeded in bringing him to a halt.

Eradicate climbed slowly down from the seat, and limped around until he stood in front of his pet.

"Yo'—yo're a nice one, ain't yo'?" he demanded in sarcastic tones. "Yo' done enough runnin' in a few minutes fo' a week ob Sundays, an' now I won't be able t' git a move out ob ye! I'se ashamed ob yo', dat's what I is! Puffickly ashamed ob yo'. Go 'long, now, an' yo' won't git no oats dish yeah day! No sah!" and, highly indignant, Eradicate led the now slowly-ambling mule off to the stable.

"I won't shoot again until you have him shut up, Rad!" laughed Tom. "I didn't know you were so close when I set off those guns."

"Dat's all right, Massa Tom," was the reply. "I done called t' you t' wait, but yo' didn't heah me, I 'spects. But it doan't mattah, now. Shoot all yo' laik, Boomerang won't run any mo' dis week. He done runned his laigs off now. Shoot away!"

But Tom was not quite ready to do this. He wanted to see what effect the first shots had had on his aerial warship, and to learn whether or not the newly devised recoil check had done what was expected of it.

"No more shooting right away," called the young inventor. "I want to see how we made out with the first round. How did she check up, Ned?"

"Fine, as far as I can tell."

"Yes, indeed," added Lieutenant Marbury. "The recoil was hardly noticeable, though, of course, with the full battery of guns in use, it might be more so."

"I hope not," answered Tom. "I haven't used the full strength of the recoil check yet. I can tune it up more, and when I do, and when I have it attached to all the guns, big and little, I think we'll do the trick. But now for a harder test."

The rest of that day was spent in trying out the guns, firing them with practice and service charges, though none of the shells used contained projectiles. It would not have been possible to shoot these, with the Mars held in place in the midst of Tom's factory buildings.

"Well, is she a success, Tom?" asked Ned, when the experimenting was over for the time being.

"I think I can say so—yes," was the answer, with a questioning look at the officer.

"Indeed it is—a great success! We must give the Newton shock absorber due credit."

Ned blushed with pleasure.

"It was only my suggestion," he said. "Tom worked it all out."

"But I needed the suggestion to start with," the young inventor replied.

"Of course something may develop when you take your craft high in the air, and discharge the guns there," said the lieutenant. "In a rarefied atmosphere the recoil check may not be as effective as at the earth's surface. But, in such case doubtless, you can increase the strength of the springs and the hydrostatic valves."

"Yes, I counted on that," Tom explained. "I shall have to work out that formula, though, and be ready for it. But, on the whole, I am pretty well satisfied."

"And indeed you may well feel that way," commented the government official.

The Mars was hauled back into the shed, and the roof slid shut over the craft. Much yet remained to do on it, but now that Tom was sure the important item of armament was taken care of, he could devote his entire time to the finishing touches.

As his plant was working on several other pieces of machinery, some of it for the United States Government, and some designed for his own use, Tom found himself obliged to hire several new hands. An advertisement in a New York newspaper brought a large number of replies, and for a day or two Tom was kept busy sifting out the least desirable, and arranging to see those whose answers showed they knew something of the business requirements.

Meanwhile Lieutenant Marbury remained as Tom's guest, and was helpful in making suggestions that would enable the young inventor to meet the government's requirements.

"I'd like, also, to get on the track of those spies who, I am sure, wish to do you harm," said the lieutenant, "but clues seem to be scarce around here."

"They are, indeed," agreed Tom. "I guess the way in which we handled that fire in the red shed sort of discouraged them."

Lieutenant Marbury shook his head.

"They're not so easily discouraged as that," he remarked. "And, with the situation in Europe growing more acute every day, I am afraid some of those foreigners will take desperate measures to gain their ends."

"What particular ends do you mean?"

"Well, I think they will either try to so injure you that you will not be able to finish this aerial warship, or they will damage the craft itself, steal your plans, or damage some of your other inventions."

"But what object would they have in doing such a thing?" Tom wanted to know. "How would that help France, Germany or Russia, to do me an injury?"

"They are seeking to strike at the United States through you," was the answer. "They don't want Uncle Sam to have such formidable weapons as your great searchlight, the giant cannon, or this new warship of the clouds."

"But why not, as long as the United States does not intend to go to war with any of the foreign nations?" Tom inquired.

"No, it is true we do not intend to go to war with any of the conflicting European nations," admitted Lieutenant Marbury, "but you have no idea how jealous each of those foreign nations is of all the others. Each one fears that the United States will cease to be neutral, and will aid one or the other."

"Oh, so that's it?" exclaimed Tom.

"Yes, each nation, which may, at a moments notice, be drawn into a war with one or more rival nations, fears that we may throw in our lot with its enemies."

"And, to prevent that, they want to destroy some of my inventions?" asked Tom.

"That's the way I believe it will work out. So you must be careful, especially since you have taken on so many new men."

"That's so," agreed the young inventor. "I have had to engage more strangers than ever before, for I am anxious to get the Mars finished and give it a good test. And, now that you have mentioned it, there are some of those men of whom I am a bit suspicious."

"Have they done anything to make you feel that way?" asked the lieutenant.

"Well, not exactly; it is more their bearing, and the manner in which they go about the works. I must keep my eye on them, for it takes only a few discontented men to spoil a whole shop full. I will be on my guard."

"And not only about your new airship and other inventions," said the officer, "but about yourself, personally. Will you do that?"

"Yes, though I don't imagine anything like that will happen."

"Well, be on your guard, at all events," warned Lieutenant Marbury.

As Tom had said, he had been obliged to hire a number of new men. Some of these were machinists who had worked for him, or his father, on previous occasions, and, when tasks were few, had been dismissed, to go to other shops. These men, Tom felt sure, could be relied upon.

But there were a number of others, from New York, and other large cities, of whom Tom was not so sure.

"You have more foreigners than I ever knew you to hire before, Tom," his father said to him one day, coming back from a tour of the shops.

"Yes, I have quite a number," Tom admitted. "But they are all good workmen. They stood the test."

"Yes, some of them are too good," observed the older inventor. "I saw one of them making up a small motor the other day, and he was winding the armature a new way. I spoke to him about it, and he tried to prove that his way was an improvement on yours. Why, he'd have had it short-circuited in no time if I hadn't stopped him."

"Is that so?" asked Tom. "That is news to me. I must look into this."

"Are any of the new men employed on the Mars?" Mr. Swift asked.

"No, not yet, but I shall have to shift some there from other work I think, in order to get finished on time."

"Well, they will bear watching I think," his father said.

"Why, have you seen anything—do you—" began the young man, for Mr. Swift had not been told of the suspicions of the lieutenant.

"Oh, it isn't anything special," the older inventor went on. "Only I wouldn't let a man I didn't know much about get too much knowledge of my latest invention."

"I won't, Dad. Thanks for telling me. This latest craft is sure going to be a beauty."

"Then you think it will work, Tom?"

"I'm sure of it, Dad!"

Mr. Swift shook his head in doubt.

CHAPTER XI
A DAY OFF

Tom Swift pondered long and intently over what his father had said to him. He sat for several minutes in his private office, after the aged inventor had passed out, reviewing in his mind the talk just finished.

"I wonder," said Tom slowly, "if any of the new men could have obtained work here for the purpose of furthering that plot the lieutenant suspects? I wonder if that could be true?"

And the more Tom thought of it, the more he was convinced that such a thing was at least possible.

"I must make a close inspection, and weed out any suspicious characters," he decided, "though I need every man I have working now, to get the Mars finished in time. Yes, I must look into this."

Tom had reached a point in his work where he could leave much to his helpers. He had several good foremen, and, with his father to take general supervision over more important details, the young inventor had more time to himself. Of course he did not lay too many burdens on his father's shoulders since Mr. Swift's health was not of the best.

But Tom's latest idea, the aerial warship, was so well on toward completion that his presence was not needed in that shop more than two or three times a day.

"When I'm not there I'll go about in the other shops, and sort of size up the situation," he decided. "I may be able to get a line on some of those plotters, if there are any here."

Lieutenant Marbury had departed for a time, to look after some personal matters, but he was to return inside of a week, when it was hoped to give the aerial warship its first real test in flight, and under some of the conditions that it would meet with in actual warfare.

As Tom was about to leave his office, to put into effect his new resolution to make a casual inspection of the other shops, he met Koku, the giant, coming in. Koku's hands and face were black with oil and machine filings.

"Well, what have you been doing?" Tom wanted to know. "Did you have an accident?" For Koku had no knowledge of machinery, and could not even be trusted to tighten up a simple nut by himself. But if some one stood near him, and directed him how to apply his enormous strength, Koku could do more than several machines.

"No accident, Master," he replied. "I help man lift that hammer-hammer thing that pounds so. It get stuck!"

"What, the hammer of the drop forger?" cried Tom. "Was that out of order again?"

"Him stuck," explained Koku simply.

There was an automatic trip-hammer in one of the shops, used for pounding out drop forgings, and this hammer seemed to take especial delight in getting out of order. Very often it jammed, or "stuck," as Koku described it, and if the hammer could not be forced back on the channel or upright guide-plates, it meant that it must be taken apart, and valuable time lost. Once Koku had been near when the hammer got out of order, and while the workmen were preparing to dismantle it, the giant seized the big block of steel, and with a heave of his mighty shoulders forced it back on the guides.

"And is that what you did this time?" asked Tom.

"Yes, Master. Me fix hammer," Koku answered. "I get dirty, I no care. Man say I no can fix. I show him I can!"

"What man said that?"

"Man who run hammer. Ha! I lift him by one finger! He say he no like to work on hammer. He want to work on airship. I tell him I tell you, maybe you give him job—he baby! Koku can work hammer. Me fix it when it get stuck."

"Well, maybe you know what you're talking about, but I don't," said Tom, with a pleasant smile at his big helper. "Come on, Koku, we'll go see what it all means."

"Koku work hammer, maybe?" asked the giant hope fully.

"Well, I'll see," half promised Tom. "If it's going to get out of gear all the while it might pay me to keep you at it so you could get it back in place whenever it kicked up a fuss, and so save time. I'll see about it."

Koku led the way to the shop where the triphammer was installed. It was working perfectly now, as Tom could tell by the thundering blows it struck. The man operating it looked up as Tom approached, and, at a gesture from the young inventor, shut off the power.

"Been having trouble here?" asked Tom, noting that the workman was one of the new hands he had hired.

"Yes, sir, a little," was the respectful answer. "This hammer goes on a strike every now and then, and gets jammed. Your giant there forced it back into place, which is more than I could do with a big bar for a lever. He sure has some muscle."

"Yes," agreed Tom, "he's pretty strong. But what's this you said about wanting to give up this job, and go on the airship construction."

The man turned red under his coat of grime.

"I didn't intend him to repeat that to you, Mr. Swift," he said. "I was a little put out at the way this hammer worked. I lose so much time at it that I said I'd like to be transferred to the airship department. I've worked in one before. But I'm not making a kick," he added quickly. "Work is too scarce for that."

"I understand," said Tom. "I have been thinking of making a change. Koku seems to like this hammer, and knows how to get it in order once it gets off the guides. You say you have had experience in airship construction?"

"Yes, sir. I've worked on the engines, and on the planes."

"Know anything about dirigible balloons?"

"Yes, I've worked on them, too, but the engineering part is my specialty. I'm a little out of my element on a trip-hammer."

"I see. Well, perhaps I'll give you a trial. Meanwhile you might break Koku in on operating this machine. If I transfer you I'll put him on this hammer."

"Thank you, Mr. Swift! I'll show him all I know about it. Oh, there goes the hammer again!" he exclaimed, for, as he started it up, as Tom turned away, the big piece of steel once more jammed on the channel-plates.

"Me fix!" exclaimed the giant eagerly, anxious for a chance to exhibit his great strength.

"Wait a minute!" exclaimed Tom. "I want to get a look at that machine."

He inspected it carefully before he signaled for Koku to force the hammer back into place. But, if Tom saw anything suspicious, he said nothing. There was, however, a queer look on his face as he turned aside, and he murmured to himself, as he walked away:

"So you want to be transferred to the airship department, do you? Well, we'll see about that. We'll see."

Tom had more problems to solve than those of making an aerial warship that would be acceptable to the United States Government.

Ned Newton called on his chum that evening. The two talked of many things, gradually veering around to the subject uppermost in Tom's mind—his new aircraft.

"You're thinking too much of that." Ned warned him. "You're as bad as the time you went for your first flight."

"I suppose I am," admitted Tom. "But the success of the Mars means a whole lot to me. And that's something I nearly forgot. I've got to go out to the shop now. Want to come along, Ned?"

"Sure, though I tell you that you're working too hard—burning the electric light at both ends."

"This is just something simple," Tom said. "It won't take long."

He went out, followed by his chum.

"But this isn't the way to the airship shed," objected the young bank clerk, as he noted in which direction Tom was leading him.

"I know it isn't," Tom replied. "But I want to look at one of the trip-hammers in the forge shop when none of the men is around. I've been having a little trouble there."

"Trouble!" exclaimed his chum. "Has that plot Lieutenant Marbury spoke of developed?"

"Not exactly. This is something else," and Tom told of the trouble with the big hammer.

"I had an idea," the young inventor said, "that the man at the machine let it get out of order purposely, so I'd change him. I want to see if my suspicions are correct."

Tom carefully inspected the hammer by the light of a powerful portable electric lamp Ned held.

"Ha! There it is!" Tom suddenly exclaimed.

"Something wrong?" Ned inquired.

"Yes. This is what's been throwing the hammer off the guides all the while," and Tom pulled out a small steel bolt that had been slipped into an oil hole. A certain amount of vibration, he explained to Ned, would rattle the bolt out so that it would force the hammer to one side, throwing it off the channel-plates, and rendering it useless for the time being.

"A foxy trick," commented Tom. "No wonder the machine got out of kilter so easily."

"Do you think it was done purposely?"

"Well, I'm not going to say. But I'm going to watch that man. He wants to be transferred to the airship department. He put this in the hammer, perhaps, to have an excuse for a change. Well, I'll give it to him."

"You don't mean that you'd take a fellow like that and put him to work on your new aerial warship, do you, Tom?"

"Yes, I think I will, Ned. You see, I look at it this way: I haven't any real proof against him now. He could only laugh at me if I accused him. But you've heard the proverb about giving a calf rope enough and he'll hang himself, haven't you?"

"I think I have."

"Well, I'm going to give this fellow a little rope. I'll transfer him, as he asks, and I'll keep a close watch on him."

"But won't it be risky?"

"Perhaps, but no more so than leaving him in here to work mischief. If he is hatching a plot, the sooner it's over with the better I shall like it. I don't like a shot to hang fire. I'm warned now, and I'll be ready for him. I have a line on whom to suspect. This is the first clue," and Tom held up the incriminating bolt.

"I think you're taking too big a risk, Tom," his chum said. "Why not discharge the man?"

"Because that might only smooth things over for a time. If this plot is being laid the sooner it comes to a head, and breaks, the better. Have it done, short, sharp and quick, is my motto. Yes, I'll shift him in the morning. Oh, but I wish it was all over, and the Mars was accepted by Uncle Sam!" and Tom put his hand to his head with a tired gesture.

"Say, old man!" exclaimed Ned, "what you want is a day off, and I'm going to see that you get it. You need a little vacation."

"Perhaps I do," assented Tom wearily.

"Then you'll have it!" cried Ned. "There's going to be a little picnic to-morrow. Why can't you go with Mary Nestor? She'd like you to take her, I'm sure. Her cousin, Helen Randall, is on from New York, and she wants to go, also."

"How do you know?" asked Tom quickly.

"Because she said so," laughed Ned. "I was over to the house to call. I have met Helen before, and I suggested that you and I would take the two girls, and have a day off. You'll come, won't you?"

"Well, I don't know," spoke Tom slowly. "I ought to—"

"Nonsense! Give up work for one day!" urged Ned. "Come along. It'll do you good—get the cobwebs out of your head."

"All right, I'll go," assented Tom, after a moment's thought.

The next day, having instructed his father and the foremen to look well to the various shops, and having seen that the work on the new aerial warship was progressing favorably, Tom left for a day's outing with his chum and the two girls.

The picnic was held in a grove that surrounded a small lake, and after luncheon the four friends went for a ride in a launch Tom hired. They went to the upper end of the lake, in rather a pretty but lonesome locality.

"Tom, you look tired," said Mary. "I'm sure you've been working too hard!"

"Why, I'm not working any harder than usual," Tom insisted.

"Yes, he is, too!" declared Ned, "and he's running more chances, too."

"Chances?" repeated Mary.

"Oh, that's all bosh!" laughed Tom. "Come on, let's go ashore and walk."

"That suits me," spoke Ned. Helen and Mary assented, and soon the four young persons were strolling through the shady wood.

After a bit the couples became separated, and Tom found himself walking beside Mary in a woodland path. The girl glanced at her companion's face, and ventured:

"A penny for your thoughts, Tom."

"They're worth more than that," he replied gallantly. "I was thinking of—you."

"Oh, how nicely you say it!" she laughed. "But I know better! You're puzzling over some problem. Tell me, what did Ned mean when he hinted at danger? Is there any, Tom?"

"None at all," he assured her. "It's just a sort of notion—"

Mary made a sudden gesture of silence.

"Hark!" she whispered to Tom, "I heard someone mention your name then. Listen!"

CHAPTER XII
A NIGHT ALARM

Mary Nestor spoke with such earnestness, and her action in catching hold of Tom's arm to enjoin silence was so pronounced that, though he had at first regarded the matter in the light of a joke, he soon thought otherwise. He glanced from the girl's face to the dense underbrush on either side of the woodland path.

"What is it, Mary?" he asked in a whisper.

"I don't just know. I heard whispering, and thought it was the rustling of the leaves of the trees. Then someone spoke your name quite loudly. Didn't you hear it?"

Tom shook his head in negation.

"It may be Ned and his friend," he whispered, his lips close to Mary's ear.

"I think not," was her answer. "Listen; there it is again."

Distinctly then, Tom heard, from some opening in the screen of bushes, his own name spoken. "Did you hear it?" asked Mary, barely forming the words with her lips. But Tom could read their motion.

"Yes," he nodded. Then, motioning to Mary to remain where she was, he stepped forward, taking care to tread only on grassy places where there were no little twigs or branches to break and betray his presence. He was working his way toward the sound of the unseen voice.

There was a sudden movement in the bushes, just beyond the spot Tom was making for. He halted quickly and peered ahead. Mary, too, was looking on anxiously.

Tom saw the forms of two men, partially concealed by bushes, walking away from him. The men took no pains to conceal their movements, so Tom was emboldened to advance with less caution. He hurried to where he could get a good view, and, at the sight of one of the men, he uttered an exclamation.

"What is it?" asked Mary, who was now at his side. She had seen that Tom had thrown aside caution, and she had come up to join him.

"That man—I know him!" the young inventor exclaimed. "It is Feldman—the one who wanted to be changed from the trip-hammer to the airship department. But who is that with him?"

As Tom spoke the other turned, and at the sight of his face Mary Nestor said:

"He looks like a Frenchman, with that little mustache and imperial."

"So he is!" exclaimed Tom, in a hoarse whisper. "He must be the Frenchman that Eradicate spoke about. I wonder what this can mean? I didn't know Feldman had left the shop."

"You may know what you're talking about, but I don't, Tom," said Mary, with a smile at her companion. "Are they friends of yours?"

"Hardly," spoke the young inventor dryly. "That one, Feldman, is one of my workmen. He had charge of a drop-forge press and trip-hammer that—"

"Spare me the details, Tom!" interrupted Mary. "You know I don't understand a thing about machinery. The wireless you erected on Earthquake Island was as much as I could comprehend."

"Well, a trip-hammer isn't as complicated as that," spoke Tom, with a laugh, as he noticed that the two men were far enough away so they could not hear him. "What I was going to say was, that one of those men works in our shops. The other I don't know, but I agree with you that he does look like a Frenchman, and old Eradicate had a meeting with a man whom he described as being of that nationality."

"And you say they are not friends of yours?"

"I have no reason to believe they are."

"Then they must be enemies!" exclaimed Mary with quick intuition. "Oh, Tom, you will be careful, won't you?"

"Of course I will, little girl," he said, a note of fondness creeping into his voice, as he covered the small hand with his own large one. "But there is no danger."

"Then why were these men discussing you?"

"I don't know that they were, Mary."

"They mentioned your name."

"Well, that may be. Probably one of them, Feldman, who works for me, was speaking to his companion about the chance for a position. My father and I employ a number of men, you know."

"Well, I suppose it is all right, Tom, and I surely hope it is. But you will be careful, won't you? And you look more worried than you used to. Has anything gone wrong?"

"Not a thing, little girl. Everything is going fine. My new aerial warship will soon make a trial flight, and I'd be pleased to have you as a passenger."

"Would you really, Tom?"

"Of course. Consider that you have the first invitation."

"That's awfully nice of you. But you do look worried, Tom. Has anything troubled you?"

"No, not much. Everything is going all right now. We did have a little trouble at a fire in one of my buildings—"

"A fire! Oh, Tom! You never told me!"

"Well, it didn't amount to much—the only suspicious fact about it was that it seemed to have been of incendiary origin."

Mary seemed much alarmed, and again begged Tom to be on his guard, which he promised to do. Had Mary known the warnings uttered by Lieutenant Marbury she might have had more occasion for worry.

"Do you suppose that hammer man of yours came to these woods to meet that Frenchman and talk about you, Tom?" asked his companion, when the two men had strolled out of sight, and the young people were on their way back to the launch.

"Well, it's possible. I have been warned that foreign spies are trying to get hold of some of my patents, and also to hamper the government in the use of some others I have sold. But they'll have their own troubles to get away with anything. The works are pretty well guarded, and you forget I have the giant, Koku, who is almost a personal bodyguard."

"Yes, but he can't be everywhere at once. Oh, you will be careful, won't you, Tom?"

"Yes, Mary, I will," promised the young inventor. "But don't say anything to Ned about what we just saw and heard."

"Why not?"

"Because he's been at me to hire a couple of detectives to watch over me, and this would give him another excuse. Just don't say anything, and I'll adopt all the precautions I think are needful."

"I will on condition that you do that."

"And I promise I will."

With that Mary had to be content. A little later they joined Ned and his friend, and soon they were moving swiftly down the lake in the launch.

"Well, hasn't it done you good to take a day off?" Ned demanded of his chum, when they were on their homeward way.

"Yes, I think it has," agreed Tom.

"You swung your thoughts into a new channel, didn't you?"

"Oh, yes, I found something new to think about," admitted the young inventor, with a quick look at Mary.

But, though Tom thus passed off lightly the little incident of the day, he gave it serious thought when he was alone.

"Those fellows were certainly talking about me," he reasoned. "I wonder what for? And Feldman left the shop without my knowledge. I'll have to look into that. I wonder if that Frenchy looking chap I saw was the one who tried to pump Eradicate? Another point to settle."

The last was easily disposed of, for, on reaching his shops that afternoon, Tom cross-questioned the colored man, and obtained a most accurate description of the odd foreigner. It tallied in every detail with the man Tom had seen in the woods.

"And now about Feldman," mused Tom, as he went to the foreman of the shop where the suspected man had been employed.

"Yes, Feldman asked for a day off," the foreman said in response to Tom's question. "He claimed his mother was sick, and he wanted to go to see her. I knew you wouldn't object, as we were not rushed in his department."

"Oh, that's all right," said Tom quickly. "Did he say where his mother lived?"

"Over Lafayette way."

"Humph!" murmured Tom. To himself he added: "Queer that he should be near Lake Loraine, in an opposite direction from Lafayette. This will bear an investigation."

The next day Tom made it his business to pass near the hammer that was so frequently out of order. He found Feldman busy instructing Koku in its operation. Tom resolved on a little strategy.

"How is it working, Feldman?" he asked.

"Very well, Mr. Swift. There doesn't seem to be any trouble at all, but it may happen any minute. Koku seems to take to it like a duck to water."

"Well, when he is ready to assume charge let me know."

"And then am I to go into the aeroplane shop?"

"I'll see. By the way, how is your mother?" he asked quickly, looking Feldman full in the face.

"She is much better. I took a day off yesterday to go to see her," the man replied quietly enough, and without sign of embarrassment.

"That's good. Let me see, she lives over near Lake Loraine, doesn't she?"

This time Feldman could not repress a start. But he covered it admirably by stooping over to pick up a tool that fell to the floor.

"No, my mother is in Lafayette," he said. "I don't know where Lake Loraine is."

"Oh," said Tom, as he turned aside to hide a smile. He was sure now he knew at least one of the plotters.

But Tom was not yet ready to show his hand. He wanted better evidence than any he yet possessed. It would take a little more time.

Work on the aerial warship was rushed, and it seemed likely that a trial flight could be made before the date set. Lieutenant Marbury sent word that he would be on hand when needed, and in some of the shops, where fittings for the Mars were being made, night and day shifts were working.

"Well, if everything goes well, we'll take her for a trial flight to-morrow," said Tom, coming in from the shops one evening.

"Guns and all?" asked Ned, who had come over to pay his chum a visit. Mr. Damon was also on hand, invoking occasional blessings.

"Guns and all," replied Tom.

Ned had a little vacation from the bank, and was to stay all night, as was Mr. Damon.

What time it was, save that it must be near midnight, Tom could not tell, but he was suddenly awakened by hearing yells from Eradicate:

"Massa Tom! Massa Tom!" yelled the excited colored man. "Git up! Git up! Suffin' turrible am happenin' in de balloon shop. Hurry! An' yo' stan' still, Boomerang, or I'll twist yo' tail, dat's what I will! Hurry, Massa Tom!"

Tom leaped out of bed.

CHAPTER XIII
THE CAPTURE

Tom Swift was something like a fireman. He had lived so long in an atmosphere of constant alarms and danger, that he was always ready for almost any emergency. His room was equipped with the end in view that he could act promptly and effectively.

So, when he heard Eradicate's alarm, though he wondered what the old colored man was doing out of bed at that hour, Tom did not stop to reason out that puzzle. He acted quickly.

His first care was to throw on the main switch, connected with a big storage battery, and to which were attached the wires of the lighting system. This at once illuminated every shop in the plant, and also the grounds themselves. Tom wanted to see what was going on. The use of a storage battery eliminated the running of the dynamo all night.

And once he had done this, Tom began pulling on some clothes and a pair of shoes. At the same time he reached out with one hand and pressed a button that sounded an alarm in the sleeping quarters of Koku, the giant, and in the rooms of some of the older and most trusted men.

All this while Eradicate was shouting away, down in the yard.

"Massa Tom! Massa Tom!" he called. "Hurry! Hurry! Dey is killin' Koku!"

"Killing Koku!" exclaimed Tom, as he finished his hasty dressing. "Then my giant must already be in the fracas. I wonder what it's all about, anyhow."

"What's up, Tom?" came Ned's voice from the adjoining room. "I thought I heard a noise."

"Your thoughts do you credit, Ned!" Tom answered. "If you listen right close, you'll hear several noises."

"By Jove! You're right, old man!"

Tom could hear his chum bound out of bed to the floor, and, at the same time, from the big shed where Tom was building his aerial warship came a series of yells and shouts.

"That's Koku's voice!" Tom exclaimed, as he recognized the tones of the giant.

"I'm coming, Tom!" Ned informed his chum. "Wait a minute."

"No time to wait," Tom replied, buttoning his coat as he sped down the hall.

"Oh, Tom, what is it?" asked Mrs. Baggert, the housekeeper, looking from her room.

"I don't know. But don't let dad get excited, no matter what happens. Just put him off until I come back. I think it isn't anything serious."

Mr. Damon, who roomed next to Ned, came out of his own apartment partially dressed.

"Bless my suspenders!" he cried to Tom, those articles just then dangling over his hips. "What is it? What has happened? Bless my steam gauge, don't tell me it's a fire!"

"I think it isn't that," Tom answered. "No alarm has rung. Koku seems to be in trouble."

"Well, he's big enough to look after himself, that's one consolation," chuckled Mr. Damon. "I'll be right with you."

By this time Ned had run out into the hall, and, together, he and Tom sped down the corridor. They could not hear the shouts of Eradicate so plainly now, as he was on the other side of the house.

But when the two young men reached the front porch, they could hear the yells given with redoubled vigor. And, in the glare of the electric lights, Tom saw Eradicate leading along Boomerang, the old mule.

"What is it, Rad? What is it?" demanded the young inventor breathlessly.

"Trouble, Massa Tom! Dat's what it am! Trouble!"

"I know that—but what kind?"

"De worstest kind, I 'spects, Massa Tom. Listen to it!"

From the interior of the big shed, not far from the house, Tom and Ned heard a confused jumble of shouts, cries and pleadings, mingled with the rattle of pieces of metal, and the banging of bits of wood. And, above all that, like the bellowing of a bull, was noted the rumbling voice of Koku, the giant.

"Come on, Ned!" Tom cried.

"It's suah trouble, all right," went on Eradicate. "Mah mule, Boomerang, had a touch ob de colic, an' I got up t' gib him some hot drops an' walk him around, when I heard de mostest terrific racket-sound, and den I 'spected trouble was comm."

"It isn't coming—it's here!" called Tom, as he sped toward the big shop. Ned was but a step behind him. The big workshop where the aerial warship was being built was, like the other buildings, brilliantly illuminated by the lights Tom had switched on. The young inventor also saw several of his employees speeding toward the same point.

Tom was the first to reach the small door of the shed. This was built in one of the two large main doors, which could be swung open when it was desired to slide the Mars in from the ground, and not admit it through the roof.

"Look!" cried Tom, pointing.

Ned looked over his chum's shoulder and saw the giant, Koku, struggling with four men—powerful men they were, too, and they seemed bent on mischief.

For they came at Koku from four sides, seeking to hold his hands and feet so that he could not fight them back. On the floor near where the struggle was taking place was a coil of rope, and it was evident that it had been the intention of the men to overcome Koku and truss him up, so that he would not interfere with what they intended to do. But Koku was a match for even the four men, powerful as they were.

"We're here, Koku!" cried Tom. "Watch for an opening, Ned!" he called to his chum.

The sound of Tom's voice disconcerted at least two of the attackers, for they looked around quickly, and this was fatal to their chances.

Though such a big man, Koku was exceptionally quick, and no sooner did he see his advantage, as two of the men turned their gaze away from him, than he seized it.

Suddenly tearing loose his hands from the grip of the two men who had looked around, Koku shot out his right and left fists, and secured good hold on the necks of two of his enemies. The other two, at his back, were endeavoring to pull him over, but the giant's sturdy legs still held.

So big was Koku's hands that they almost encircled the necks of his antagonists. Then happened a curious thing.

With a shout that might have done credit to some ancient cave-dweller of the stone age, Koku spread out his mighty arms, and held apart the two men he had grasped. In vain they struggled to free themselves from that terrible grip. Their faces turned purple, and their eyes bulged out.

"He's choking them to death!" shouted Ned.

But Koku was not needlessly cruel.

A moment later, with a quick and sudden motion he bent his arms, bringing toward each other the two men he held as captives. Their heads came together with a dull thud, and a second later Koku allowed two limp bodies to slip from his grip to the floor.

"He's done for them!" Tom cried. "Knocked them unconscious. Good for you, Koku!"

The giant grunted, and then, with a quick motion, slung himself around, hoping to bring the enemies at his back within reach of his powerful arms. But there was no need of this.

As soon as the other two ruffians had seen their companions fall to the floor of the shop they turned and fled, leaping from an open window.

"There they go!" cried Ned.

"Some of the other men can chase them," said the young inventor. "We'll tie up the two Koku has captured."

As he approached nearer to the unconscious captives Tom uttered a cry of surprise, for he recognized them as two of the new men he had employed.

"What can this mean?" he asked wonderingly.

He glanced toward the window through which the two men had jumped to escape, and he was just in time to see one of them run past the open door. The face of this one was under a powerful electric light, and Tom at once recognized the man as Feldman, the worker who had had so much trouble with the trip-hammer.

"This sure is a puzzle," marveled Tom. "My own men in the plot! But why did they attack Koku?"

The giant, bending over the men he had knocked unconscious by beating their heads together, seemed little worse for the attack.

"We tie 'em up," he said grimly, as he brought over the rope that had been intended for himself.

CHAPTER XIV
THE FIRST FLIGHT

Little time was lost in securing the two men who had been so effectively rendered helpless by Koku's ready, if rough, measures. One of them was showing signs of returning consciousness now, and Tom, not willing to inflict needless pain, even on an enemy, told one of his men, summoned by the alarm, to bring water. Soon the two men opened their eyes, and looked about them in dazed fashion.

"Did—did anything hit me?" asked one meekly.

"It must have been a thunderbolt," spoke the other dreamily. "But it didn't look like a storm."

"Oh, dere was a storm, all right," chuckled Eradicate, who, having left his mule, Boomerang outside, came into the shed. "It was a giant storm all right."

The men put their hands to their heads, and seemed to comprehend. They looked at the rope that bound their feet. Their forearms had been loosened to allow them to take a drink of water.

"What does this mean—Ransom—Kurdy?" asked Tom sternly, when the men seemed able to talk. "Did you attack Koku?"

"It looks as though he had the best of us, whether we did or not," said the man Tom knew as Kurdy. "Whew, how my head aches!"

"Me sorry," said Koku simply.

"Not half as sorry as we are," returned Ransom ruefully.

"What does it mean?" asked Tom sternly. "There were four of you. Feldman and one other got away."

"Oh, trust Feldman for getting away," sneered Kurdy. "He always leaves his friends in the lurch."

"Was this a conspiracy?" demanded Tom.

The two captives looked at one another, sitting bound on the floor of the shop, their backs against some boxes.

"I guess it's all up, and we might as well make a clean breast of it," admitted Kurdy.

"Perhaps it would be better," said Tom quietly. "Eradicate," he went on, to the colored man, "go to the house and tell Mrs. Baggert that everything is all right and no one hurt."

"No one hurt, Massa Tom? What about dem dere fellers?" and the colored man pointed to the captives.

"Well, they're not hurt much," and Tom permitted himself a little smile. "I don't want my father to worry. Tell him everything is all right."

"All right, Massa Tom. I'se gwine right off. I'se got t' look after mah mule, Boomerang, too. I'se gwine," and he shuffled away.

"Who else besides Feldman got away?" asked Tom, looking alternately at the prisoners.

They hesitated a moment about answering.

"We might as well give up, I tell you," spoke Kurdy to Ransom.

"All right, go ahead, we'll have to take our medicine. I might have known it would turn out this way—going in for this sort of thing. It's the first bit of crooked business I ever tried," the man said earnestly, "and it will be the last—believe me!"

"Who was the fourth man?" Tom repeated.

"Harrison," answered Kurdy, naming one of the most efficient of the new machinists Tom had hired during the rush.

"Harrison, who has been working on the motor?" cried the young inventor.

"Yes," said Ransom.

"I'm sorry to learn that," Tom went on in a low voice. "He was an expert in his line. But what was your object, anyhow, in attacking Koku?"

"We didn't intend to attack him," explained Ransom, "but he came in when we were at work, and as he went for us we tried to stand him off. Then your colored man heard the racket, and—well, I guess you know the rest."

"But I don't understand why you came into this shed at night," went on Tom. "No one is allowed in here. You had no right, and Koku knew that. What did you want?"

"Look here!" exclaimed Kurdy, "I said we'd make a clean breast of it, and we will. We're only a couple of tools, and we were foolish ever to go in with those fellows; or rather, in with that Frenchman, who promised us big money if we succeeded."

"Succeeded in what?" demanded the young inventor.

"In damaging your new aerial warship, or in getting certain parts of it so he could take them away with him."

Tom gave a surprised whistle.

"A frenchman!" he exclaimed. "Is he one of the—?"

"Yes, he's one of the foreign spies," interrupted Ransom. "You'd find it out, anyhow, if we didn't tell you. They are after you, Tom Swift, and after your machines. They had vowed to get them by fair means or foul, for some of the European governments are desperate."

"But we were only tools in their hands. So were Feldman and Harrison, but they knew more about the details. We were only helping them."

"Then we must try to capture them," decided Tom. "Ned, see if the chase had any results. I'll look after these chaps—Koku and I."

"Oh, we give in," admitted Kurdy. "We know when we've had enough," and he rubbed his head gently where the giant had banged it against that of his fellow-conspirator.

"Do you mean that you four came into this shop, at midnight, to damage the Mars?" asked Tom.

"That's about it, Mr. Swift," replied Kurdy rather shamefacedly. "We were to damage it beyond repair, set fire to the whole place, if need be, and, at the same time, take away certain vital parts.

"Harrison, Feldman, Ransom and I came in, thinking the coast was clear. But Koku must have seen us enter, or he suspected we were here, for he came in after us, and the fight began. We couldn't stop him, and he did for us. I'm rather glad of it, too, for I never liked the work. It was only that they tempted me with a promise of big money."

"Who tempted you?" demanded Tom.

"That Frenchman—La Foy, he calls himself, and some other foreigners in your shops."

"Are there foreigners here?" cried Tom.

"Bless my chest protector!" cried Mr. Damon, who had come in and had been a silent listener to this. "Can it be possible?"

"That's the case," went on Kurdy. "A lot of the new men you took on are foreign spies from different European nations. They are trying to learn all they can about your plans, Mr. Swift!"

"Are they friendly among themselves?" asked Tom.

"No; each one is trying to get ahead of the other. So far the Frenchman seems to have had the best of it. But to-night his plan failed."

"Tell me more about it," urged Tom.

"That's about all we know," spoke Ransom. "We were only hired to do the rough work. Those higher up didn't appear. Feldman was only a step above us."

"Then my suspicions of him were justified," thought Tom. "He evidently met La Foy in the woods to make plans. But Koku and Eradicate spoiled them."

The two captives seemed willing enough to make a confession, but they did not know much. As they said, they were merely tools, acting for others. And events had happened just as they had said.

The four conspirators had managed, by means of a false key, and by disconnecting the burglar alarm, to enter the airship shed. They were about to proceed with their work of destruction when Koku came on the scene.

The giant's appearance was due to accident. He acted as a sort of night watchman, making a tour of the buildings, but he entered the shed where the Mars was because, that day, he had left his knife in there, and wanted to get it. Only for that he would not have gone in. When he entered he surprised the four men.

Of course he attacked them at once, and they sprang at him. Then ensued a terrific fight. Eradicate, arising to doctor his mule, as he had said, heard the noise, and saw what was going on. He gave the alarm.

"Well, Ned, any luck?" asked Tom, as his chum came in.

"No, they got away, Tom. I had a lot of your men out helping me search the grounds, but it wasn't of much use."

"Particularly if you depended on some of my men," said Tom bitterly.

"What do you mean?"

"I mean that the place is filled with spies, Ned! But we will sift them out in the morning. This has been a lucky night for me. It was touch and go. Now, then, Koku, take these fellows and lock them up somewhere until morning. Ned, you and I will remain on guard here the rest of the night."

"I'm with you, Tom."

"Will you be a bit easy on us, considering what we told you?" asked Kurdy.

"I'll do the best I can," said Tom, gently, making no promises.

The two captives were put in secure quarters, and the rest of the night passed quietly. During the fight in the airship shed some machinery and tools had been broken, but no great amount of damage was done. Tom and Ned passed the remaining hours of darkness there.

A further search was made in the morning for the two conspirators who had escaped, but no trace of them was found. Tom then realized why Feldman was so anxious to be placed in the aeroplane department—it was in order that he might have easier access to the Mars.

A technical charge was made against the two prisoners, sufficient to hold them for some time. Then Tom devoted a day to weeding out the suspected foreigners in his place. All the new men were discharged, though some protested against this action.

"Probably I am hitting some of the innocent in punishing those who, if they had the chance, would become guilty," Tom said to his chum, "but it cannot be helped—I can't afford to take any chances."

The Mars was being put in shape for her first flight. The guns, fitted with the recoil shock absorbers, were mounted, and Lieutenant Marbury had returned to go aloft in the big aerial warship. He congratulated Tom on discovering at least one plot in time.

"But there may be more," he warned the young inventor. "You are not done with them yet."

The Mars was floated out of her hangar, and made ready for an ascent. Tom, Ned, Lieutenant Marbury, Mr. Damon, and several workmen were to be the first passengers. Tom was busy going over the various parts to see that nothing had been forgotten.

"Well, I guess we're ready," he finally announced. "All aboard!"

"Bless my insurance policy!" exclaimed Mr. Damon. "Now that the time comes I almost wish I wasn't going."

"Nonsense!" exclaimed Tom. "You're not going to back out at the last minute. All aboard! Cast off the ropes!" he cried to the assistants.

A moment later the Mars, the biggest airship Tom Swift had ever constructed, arose from the earth like some great bird, and soared aloft.

CHAPTER XV
IN DANGER

"Well, Tom, we're moving!" cried Ned Newton, clapping his chum on the back, as he stood near him in the pilot-house. "We're going up, old sport!"

"Of course we are," replied Tom. "You didn't think it wouldn't go up, did you?"

"Well, I wasn't quite sure," Ned confessed. "You know you were so worried about—"

"Not about the ship sailing," interrupted Tom. "It was only the effect the firing of the guns might have. But I think we have that taken care of."

"Bless my pin cushion!" cried Mr. Damon, as he looked over the rail at the earth below. "We're moving fast, Tom."

"Yes, we can make a quicker ascent in this than in most aeroplanes," Tom said, "for they have to go up in a slanting direction. But we can't quite equal their lateral speed."

"Just how fast do you think you can travel when you are in first-class shape?" asked Lieutenant Marbury, as he noted how the Mars was behaving on this, the first trip.

"Well, I set a limit of seventy-five miles an hour," the young inventor replied, as he shifted various levers and handles, to change the speed of the mechanism. "But I'm afraid we won't quite equal that with all our guns on board. But I'm safe in saying sixty, I think."

"That will more than satisfy the government requirements," the officer said. "But, of course, your craft will have to come up to expectations and requirements in the matter of armament."

"I'll give you every test you want," declared Tom, with a smile. "And now we'll see what the Mars can do when put to it."

Up and up went the big dirigible aerial warship. Had you been fortunate enough to have seen her you would have observed a craft not unlike, in shape, the German Zeppelins. But it differed from those war balloons in several important particulars.

Tom's craft was about six hundred feet long, and the diameter of the gas bag, amidships, was sixty feet, slightly larger than the largest Zeppelin. Below the bag, which, as I have explained, was made up of a number of gas-tight compartments, hung from wire cables three cabins. The forward one was a sort of pilot-house, containing various instruments for navigating the ship of the air, observation rooms, gauges for calculating firing ranges, and the steering apparatus.

Amidships, suspended below the great bag, were the living and sleeping quarters, where food was cooked and served and where those who operated the craft could spend their leisure time. Extra supplies were also stored there.

At the stern of the big bag was the motor-room, where gas was generated to fill the balloon compartments when necessary, where the gasoline and electrical apparatus were installed, and where the real motive power of the craft was located. Here, also, was carried the large quantity of gasoline and oil needed for a long voyage. The Mars could carry sufficient fuel to last for over a week, provided no accidents occurred.

There was also an arrangement in the motor compartment, so that the ship could be steered and operated from there. This was in case the forward pilot-house should be shot away by an enemy. And, also, in the motor compartment were the sleeping quarters for the crew.

All three suspended cabins were connected by a long covered runway, so that one could pass from the pilot-house to the motor-room and back again through the amidship cabin.

At the extreme end of the big bag were the various rudders and planes, designed to keep the craft on a level keel, automatically, and to enable it to make headway against a strong wind. The motive power consisted of three double-bladed wooden propellers, which could be operated together or independently. A powerful gasoline engine was the chief motive power, though there was an auxiliary storage battery, which would operate an electrical motor and send the ship along for more than twenty-four hours in case of accident to the gasoline engine.

There were many other pieces of apparatus aboard, some not completely installed, the uses of which I shall mention from time to time, as the story progresses. The gas-generating machine was of importance, for there would be a leakage and shrinking of the vapor from the big bag, and some means must be provided for replenishing it.

"You don't seem to have forgotten anything, Tom," said Ned admiringly, as they soared upward.

"We can tell better after we've flown about a bit," observed the young inventor, with a smile. "I expect we shall have to make quite a number of changes."

"Are you going far?" asked Mr. Damon.

"Why, you're not frightened, are you?" inquired Tom. "You have been up in airships with me before."

"Oh, no, I'm not frightened!" exclaimed the odd man. "Bless my suspenders, no! But I promised my wife I'd be back this evening, and..."

"We'll sail over toward Waterford," broke in Tom, "and I'll drop you down in your front yard."

"No, don't do that! Don't! I beg of you!" cried Mr. Damon. "You see—er—Tom, my wife doesn't like me to make these trips. Of course, I understand there is no danger, and I like them. But it's just as well not to make her worry-you understand!"

"Oh, all right," replied Tom, with a laugh. "Well, we're not going far on this trip. What I want to do, most of all, is to test the guns, and see if the recoil check will work as well when we are aloft as it did down on the ground. You know a balloon isn't a very stable base for a gun, even one of light caliber."

"No, it certainly is not," agreed Lieutenant Marbury, "and I am interested in seeing how you will overcome the recoil."

"We'll have a test soon," announced Tom.

Meanwhile the Mars, having reached a considerable height, being up so far, in fact, that the village of Shopton could scarcely be distinguished, Tom set the signal that told the engine-room force to start the propellers. This would send them ahead.

Some of Tom's most trusted workmen formed the operating crew, the young inventor taking charge of the pilot-house himself.

"Well she seems to run all right," observed Lieutenant Marbury, as the big craft surged ahead just below a stratum of white, fleecy clouds.

"Yes, but not as fast as I'd like to see her go," Tom replied. "Of course the machinery is new, and it will take some little time for it to wear down smooth. I'll speed her up a little now."

They had been running for perhaps ten minutes when Tom shoved over the hand of an indicator that communicated with the engine-room from the pilot-house. At once the Mars increased her speed.

"She can do it!" cried Ned.

"Bless my-hat! I should say so!" cried Mr. Damon, for he was standing outside the pilot-house just then, on the "bridge," and the sudden increase of speed lifted his hat from his head.

"There you are—caught on the fly!" cried Ned, as he put up his hand just in time to catch the article in question.

"Thanks! Guess I'd better tie it fast," remarked the odd man, putting his hat on tightly.

The aerial warship was put through several evolutions to test her stability, and to each one she responded well, earning the praise of the government officer. Up and down, to one side and the other, around in big circles, and even reversing, Tom sent his craft with a true hand and eye. In a speed test fifty-five miles was registered against a slight wind, and the young inventor said he knew he could do better than that as soon as some of the machinery was running more smoothly.

"And now suppose we get ready for the gun tests," suggested Tom, when they had been running for about an hour.

"That's what I'm mostly interested in," said Lieutenant Marbury. "It's easy enough to get several good types of dirigible balloons, but few of them will stand having a gun fired from them, to say nothing of several guns."

"Well, I'm not making any rash promises," Tom went on, "but I think we can turn the trick."

The armament of the Mars was located around the center cabin. There were two large guns, fore and aft, throwing a four-inch projectile, and two smaller calibered quick-firers on either beam. The guns were mounted on pedestals that enabled the weapons to fire in almost any direction, save straight up, and of course the balloon bag being above them prevented this. However, there was an arrangement whereby a small automatic quick-firer could be sent up to a platform built on top of the gas envelope itself, and a man stationed there could shoot at a rival airship directly overhead.

But the main deck guns could be elevated to an angle of nearly forty-five degrees, so they could take care of nearly any hostile aircraft that approached.

"But where are the bombs I heard you speaking of?" asked Ned, as they finished looking at the guns.

"Here they are," spoke Tom, as he pointed to a space in the middle of the main cabin floor. He lifted a brass plate, and disclosed three holes, covered with a strong wire netting that could be removed. "The bombs will be dropped through those holes," explained the young inventor, "being released by a magnetic control when the operator thinks he has reached a spot over the enemy's city or fortification where the most damage will be done. I'll show you how they work a little later. Now we'll have a test of some of the guns."

Tom called for some of his men to take charge of the steering and running of the Mars while he and Lieutenant Marbury prepared to fire the two larger weapons. This was to be one of the most important tests.

Service charges had been put in, though, of course, no projectiles would be used, since they were then flying over a large city not far from Shopton.

"We'll have to wait until we get out over the ocean to give a complete test, with a bursting shell," Tom said.

He and Lieutenant Marbury were beside a gun, and were about to fire it, when suddenly, from the stern of the ship, came a ripping, tearing sound, and, at the same time, confused shouts came from the crew's quarters.

"What is it?" cried Tom.

"One of the propellers!" was the answer. "It's split, and has torn a big hole in the gas bag!"

"Bless my overshoes!" cried Mr. Damon. "We're going down!"

All on board the Mars became aware of a sudden sinking sensation.

CHAPTER XVI
TOM IS WORRIED

"Steady, all!" came in even tones from Tom Swift. Not for an instant had he lost his composure. For it was an accident, that much was certain, and one that might endanger the lives of all on board.

Above the noise of the machinery in the motor room could be heard the thrashing and banging of the broken or loose propeller-blade. Just what its condition was, could not be told, as a bulge of the gas bag hid it from the view of those gathered about the gun, which was about to be fired when the alarm was given.

"We're sinking!" cried Mr. Damon. "We're going down, Tom!"

"That's nothing," was the cool answer. "It is only for a moment. Only a few of the gas compartments can be torn. There will soon enough additional gas in the others to lift us again."

And so it proved. The moment the pressure of the lifting gas in the big oiled silk and aluminum container was lowered, it started the generating machine, and enough extra gas was pumped into the uninjured compartments to compensate for the loss.

"We're not falling so fast now," observed Ned.

"No, and we'll soon stop falling altogether," calmly declared Tom. "Too bad this accident had to happen, though."

"It might have been much worse, my boy!" exclaimed the lieutenant. "That's a great arrangement of yours—the automatic gas machine."

"It's on the same principle as the air brakes of a trolley car," explained Tom, when a look at the indicators showed that the Mars had ceased falling and remained stationary in the air. Tom had also sent a signal to the engine-room to shut off the power, so that the two undamaged propellers, as well as the broken one, ceased revolving.

"In a trolley car, you see," Tom went on, when the excitement had calmed down, "as soon as the air pressure in the tanks gets below a certain point, caused by using the air for a number of applications of the brakes, it lets a magnetized bar fall, and this establishes an electrical connection, starting the air pump. The pump forces more air into the tanks until the pressure is enough to throw the pump switch out of connection, when the pump stops. I use the same thing here."

"And very clever it is," said Mr. Damon. "Do you suppose the danger is all over, Tom?"

"For the time being, yes. But we must unship that damaged propeller, and go on with the two."

The necessary orders were given, and several men from the engine-room at once began the removal of the damaged blades.

As several spare ones were carried aboard one could be put on in place of the broken one, had this been desired. But Tom thought the accident a good chance to see how his craft would act with only two-thirds of her motive force available, so he did not order the damaged propeller replaced. When it was lowered to the deck it was carefully examined.

"What made it break?" Ned wanted to know.

"That's a question I can't answer," Tom replied. "There may have been a defect in the wood, but I had it all carefully examined before I used it."

The propeller was one of the "built-up" type, with alternate layers of ash and mahogany, but some powerful force had torn and twisted the blades. The wood was splintered and split, and some jagged pieces, flying off at a tangent, so great was the centrifugal force, had torn holes in the strong gas bag.

"Did something hit it; or did it hit something?" asked Ned as he saw Tom carefully examining the broken blades.

"Hard to say. I'll have a good look at this when we get back. Just now I want to finish that gun test we didn't get a chance to start."

"You don't mean to say you're going to keep on, and with the balloon damaged; are you?" cried Mr. Damon, in surprise.

"Certainly—why not?" Tom replied. "In warfare accidents may happen, and if the Mars can't go on, after a little damage like this, what is going to happen when she's fired on by a hostile ship? Of course I'm going on!"

"Bless my necktie!" ejaculated the odd man.

"That's the way to talk!" exclaimed Lieutenant Marbury. "I'm with you."

There really was very little danger in proceeding. The Mars was just as buoyant as before, for more gas had been automatically made, and forced into the uninjured compartments of the bag. At the same time enough sand ballast had been allowed to run out to make the weight to be lifted less in proportion to the power remaining.

True, the speed would be less, with two propellers instead of three, and the craft would not steer as well, with the torn ends of the gas bag floating out behind. But this made a nearer approach to war conditions, and Tom was always glad to give his inventions the most severe tests possible.

So, after a little while, during which it was seen that the Mars was proceeding almost normally, the matter of discharging the guns was taken up again.

The weapons were all ready to fire, and when Tom had attached the pressure gauges to note how much energy was expended in the recoil, he gave the word to fire.

The two big weapons were discharged together, and for a moment after the report echoed out among the cloud masses every soul on the ship feared another accident had happened.

For the big craft rolled and twisted, and seemed about to turn turtle. Her forward progress was halted, momentarily, and a cry of fear came from several of the members of the crew, who had had only a little experience in aircraft.

"What's the matter?" cried Ned. "Something go wrong?"

"A little," admitted Tom, with a rueful look on his face. "Those recoil checks didn't work as well in practice as they did in theory."

"Are you sure they are strong enough?" asked Lieutenant Marbury.

"I thought so," spoke Tom. "I'll put more tension on the spring next time."

"Bless my watch chain!" cried Mr. Damon. "You aren't going to fire those guns again; are you, Tom?"

"Why not? We can't tell what's the matter, nor get things right without experimenting. There's no danger."

"No danger! Don't you call nearly upsetting the ship danger?"

"Oh, well, if she turns over she'll right herself again," Tom said. "The center of gravity is low, you see. She can't float in any position but right side up, though she may turn over once or twice."

"Excuse me!" said Mr. Damon firmly. "I'd rather go down, if it's all the same to you. If my wife ever knew I was here I'd never hear the last of it!"

"We'll go down soon," Tom promised. "But I must fire a couple of shots more. You wouldn't call the recoil checks a success, would you?" and the young inventor appealed to the government inspector.

"No, I certainly would not," was the prompt answer. "I am sorry, too, for they seemed to be just what was needed. Of course I understand this is not an official test, and I am not obliged to make a report of this trial. But had it been, I should have had to score against you."

"I realize that, and I'm not asking any favors, but I'll try it again with the recoil checks tightened up. I think the hydrostatic valves were open too much, also."

Preparations were now made for firing the four-inch guns once more. All this while the Mars had been speeding around in space, being about two miles up in the air. Tom's craft was not designed to reach as great an elevation as would be possible in an aeroplane, since to work havoc to an enemy's fortifications by means of aerial bombs they do not need to be dropped from a great height.

In fact, experiments in Germany have shown that bombs falling from a great height are less effective than those falling from an airship nearer the earth. For a bomb, falling from a height of two miles, acquires enough momentum to penetrate far into the earth, so that much of the resultant explosive force is expended in a downward direction, and little damage is done to the fortifications. A bomb dropped from a lower altitude, expending its force on all sides, does much more damage.

On the other hand, in destroying buildings, it has been found desirable to drop a bomb from a good height so that it may penetrate even a protected roof, and explode inside.

Once more Tom made ready to fire, this time having given the recoil checks greater resistance. But though there was less motion imparted to the airship when the guns were discharged, there was still too much for comfort, or even safety.

"Well, something's wrong, that's sure," remarked Tom, in rather disappointed tones as he noted the effect of the second shots. "If we get as much recoil from the two guns, what would happen if we fired them all at once?"

"Don't do it! Don't do it, I beg of you!" entreated Mr. Damon. "Bless my toothbrush—don't do it!"

"I won't—just at present," Tom said, ruefully. "I'm afraid I'll have to begin all over again, and proceed along new lines."

"Well, perhaps you will," said the lieutenant. "But you may invent something much better than anything you have now. There is no great rush. Take your time, and do something good."

"Oh, I'll get busy on it right away," Tom declared. "We'll go down now, and start right to work. I'm afraid, Ned, that our idea of a door-spring check isn't going to work."

"I might have known my idea wouldn't amount to anything," said the young bank clerk.

"Oh, the idea is all right," declared Tom, "but it wants modifying. There is more power to those recoils than I figured, though our first experiments seemed to warrant us in believing that we had solved the problem."

"Are you going to try the bomb-dropping device?" asked the lieutenant.

"Yes, there can't be any recoil from that," Tom said. "I'll drop a few blank ones, and see how accurate the range finders are."

While his men were getting ready for this test Tom bent over the broken propeller, looking from that to the recoil checks, which had not come up to expectations. Then he shook his head in a worried and puzzled manner.

CHAPTER XVII
AN OCEAN FLIGHT

Dropping bombs from an aeroplane, or a dirigible balloon, is a comparatively simple matter. Of course there are complications that may ensue, from the danger of carrying high explosives in the limited quarters of an airship, with its inflammable gasoline fuel, and ever-present electric spark, to the possible premature explosion of the bomb itself. But they seem to be considered minor details now.

On the other hand, while it is comparatively easy to drop a bomb from a moving aeroplane, or dirigible balloon, it is another matter to make the bomb fall just where it will do the most damage to the enemy. It is not easy to gauge distances, high up in the air, and then, too, allowance must be made for the speed of the aircraft, the ever-increasing velocity of a falling body, and the deflection caused by air currents.

The law of velocity governing falling bodies is well known. It varies, of course, according to the height, but in general a body falling freely toward the earth, as all high-school boys know, is accelerated at the rate of thirty-two feet per second. This law has been taken advantage of by the French in the present European war. The French drop from balloons, or aeroplanes, a steel dart about the size of a lead pencil, and sharpened in about the same manner. Dropping from a height of a mile or so, that dart will acquire enough velocity to penetrate a man from his head all the way through his body to his feet.

But in dropping bombs from an airship the damage intended does not so much depend on velocity. It is necessary to know how fast the bomb falls in order to know when to set the time fuse that will explode it; though some bombs will explode on concussion.

At aeroplane meets there are often bomb-dropping contests, and balls filled with a white powder (that will make a dust-cloud on falling, and so show where they strike) are used to demonstrate the birdman's accuracy.

"We'll see how our bomb-release works," Tom went on. "But we'll have to descend a bit in order to watch the effect."

"You're not going to use real bombs, are you, Tom?" asked Ned.

"Indeed not. Just chalk-dust ones for practice. Now here is where the bombs will be placed," and he pointed to the three openings in the floor of the amidship cabin. The wire nettings were taken out and one could look down through the holes to the earth below, the ground being nearer now, as Tom had let out some of the lifting gas.

"Here is the range-finder and the speed calculator," the young inventor went on as he indicated the various instruments. "The operator sits here, where he can tell when is the most favorable moment for releasing the bomb."

Tom took his place before a complicated set of instruments, and began manipulating them. One of his assistants, under the direction of Lieutenant Marbury, placed in the three openings bombs, made of light cardboard, just the size of a regular bomb, but filled with a white powder that would, on breaking, make a dust-cloud which could be observed from the airship.

"I have first to determine where I want to drop the bomb," Tom explained, "and then I have to get my distance from it on the range-finder. Next I have to know how fast I am traveling, and how far up in the air I am, to tell what the velocity of the falling bomb will attain at a certain time. This I can do by means of these instruments, some of which I have adapted from those used by the government," he said, with a nod to the officer.

"That's right—take all the information you can get," was the smiling response.

"We will now assume that the bombs are in place in the holes in the floor of the cabin," Tom went on. "As I sit here I have before me three buttons. They control the magnets that hold the bombs in place. If I press one of the buttons it breaks the electrical current, the magnet no longer has any attraction, and it releases the explosive. Now look down. I am going to try and drop a chalk bomb near that stone fence."

The Mars was then flying over a large field and a stone fence was in plain view.

"Here she goes!" cried Tom, as he made some rapid calculations from his gauge instruments. There was a little click and the chalk bomb dropped. There was a plate glass floor in part of the cabin, and through this the progress of the pasteboard bomb could be observed.

"She'll never go anywhere near the fence!" declared Ned. "You let it drop too soon, Tom!"

"Did I? You just watch. I had to allow for the momentum that would be given the bomb by the forward motion of the balloon."

Hardly had Tom spoken than a puff of white was seen on the very top of the fence.

"There it goes?" cried the lieutenant. "You did the trick, Swift!"

"Yes, I thought I would. Well, that shows my gauges are correct, anyhow. Now we'll try the other two bombs."

In succession they were released from the bottom of the cabin, at other designated objects. The second one was near a tree. It struck within five feet, which was considered good.

"And I'll let the last one down near that scarecrow in the field," said Tom, pointing to a ragged figure in the middle of a patch of corn.

Down went the cardboard bomb, and so good was the aim of the young inventor that the white dust arose in a cloud directly back of the scarecrow.

And then a queer thing happened. For the figure seemed to come to life, and Ned, who was watching through a telescope, saw a very much excited farmer looking up with an expression of the greatest wonder on his face. He saw the balloon over his head, and shook his fist at it, evidently thinking he had had a narrow escape. But the pasteboard bomb was so light that, had it hit him, he would not have been injured, though he might have been well dusted.

"Why, that was a man! Bless my pocketbook!" cried Mr. Damon.

"I guess it was," agreed Tom. "I took it for a scarecrow."

"Well, it proved the accuracy of your aim, at any rate," observed Lieutenant Marbury. "The bomb dropping device of your aerial warship is perfect—I can testify to that."

"And I'll have the guns fixed soon, so there will be no danger of a recoil, too," added Tom Swift, with a determined look on his face.

"What's next?" asked Mr. Damon, looking at his watch. "I really ought to be home, Tom."

"We're going back now, and down. Are you sure you don't want me to drop you in your own front yard, or even on your roof? I think I could manage that."

"Bless my stovepipe, no, Tom! My wife would have hysterics. Just land me at Shopton and I'll take a car home."

The damaged airship seemed little the worse for the test to which she had been subjected, and made her way at good speed in the direction of Tom's home. Several little experiments were tried on the way back. They all worked well, and the only two problems Tom had to solve were the taking care of the recoil from the guns and finding out why the propeller had broken.

A safe landing was made, and the Mars once more put away in her hangar. Mr. Damon departed for his home, and Lieutenant Marbury again took up his residence in the Swift household.

"Well, Tom, how did it go?" asked his father.

"Not so very well. Too much recoil from the guns."

"I was afraid so. You had better drop this line of work, and go at something else."

"No, Dad!" Tom cried. "I'm going to make this work. I never had anything stump me yet, and I'm not going to begin now!"

"Well, that's a good spirit to show," said the aged inventor, with a shake of his head, "but I don't believe you'll succeed, Tom."

"Yes I will, Dad! You just wait."

Tom decided to begin on the problem of the propeller first, as that seemed more simple. He knew that the gun question would take longer.

"Just what are you trying to find out, Tom?" asked Ned, a few nights later, when he found his chum looking at the broken parts of the propeller.

"Trying to discover what made this blade break up and splinter that way. It couldn't have been centrifugal force, for it wasn't strong enough."

Tom was "poking" away amid splinters, and bits of broken wood, when he suddenly uttered an exclamation, and held up something. "Look!" he cried. "I believe I've found it."

"What?" asked Ned.

"The thing that weakened the propeller. Look at this, and smell!" He held out a piece of wood toward Ned. The bank employee saw where a half-round hole had been bored in what remained of the blade, and from that hole came a peculiar odor.

"It's some kind of acid," ventured Ned.

"That's it!" cried Tom. "Someone bored a hole in the propeller, and put in some sort of receptacle, or capsule, containing a corrosive acid. In due time, which happened to be when we took our first flight, the acid ate through whatever it was contained in, and then attacked the wood of the propeller blade. It weakened the wood so that the force used in whirling it around broke it."

"Are you sure of that?" asked Ned.

"As sure as I am that I'm here! Now I know what caused the accident!"

"But who would play such a trick?" asked Ned. "We might all have been killed."

"Yes, I know we might," said Tom. "It must be the work of some of those foreign spies whose first plot we nipped in the bud. I must tell Marbury of this, but don't mention it to dad."

"I won't," promised Ned.

Lieutenant Marbury agreed with Tom that someone had surreptitiously bored a small hole in the propeller blade, and had inserted a corrosive acid that would take many hours to operate. The hole had been varnished over, probably, so it would not show.

"And that means I've got to examine the other two blades," Tom said. "They may be doctored too."

But they did not prove to be. A careful examination showed nothing wrong. An effort was made to find out who had tried to destroy the Mars in midair, but it came to nothing. The two men in custody declared they knew nothing of it, and there was no way of proving that they did.

Meanwhile, the torn gas bag was repaired, and Tom began working on the problem of doing away with the gun recoil. He tried several schemes, and almost was on the point of giving up when suddenly he received a hint by reading an account of how the recoil was taken care of on some of the German Zeppelins.

The guns there were made double, with the extra barrel filled with water or sand, that could be shot out as was the regular charge. As both barrels were fired at the same time, and in opposite directions, with the same amount of powder, one neutralized the other, and the recoil was canceled, the ship remaining steady after fire.

"By Jove! I believe that will do the trick!" cried Tom. "I'm going to try it."

"Good luck to you!" cried Ned.

It was no easy matter to change all the guns of the Mars, and fit them with double barrels. But by working day and night shifts Tom managed it.

Meanwhile, a careful watch was kept over the shops. Several new men applied for work, and some of them were suspicious enough in looks, but Tom took on no new hands.

Finally the new guns were made, and tried with the Mars held on the ground. They behaved perfectly, the shooting of sand or water from the dummy barrel neutralizing the shot from the service barrel.

"And now to see how it works in practice!" cried Tom one day. "Are you with me for a long flight, Ned?"

"I sure am!"

The next evening the Mars, with a larger crew than before, and with Tom, Ned, Mr. Damon and Lieutenant Marbury aboard, set sail.

"But why start at night?" asked Ned.

"You'll see in the morning," Tom answered.

The Mars flew slowly all night, life aboard her, at about the level of the clouds, going on almost as naturally as though the occupants of the cabins were on the earth. Excellent meals were served.

"But when are you going to try the guns?" asked Ned, as he got ready to turn in.

"Tell you in the morning," replied Tom, with a smile.

And, in the morning, when Ned looked down through the plate glass in the cabin floor, he uttered a cry.

"Why, Tom! We're over the ocean!" he cried.

"I rather thought we'd be," was the calm reply. "I told George to head straight for the Atlantic. Now we'll have a test with service charges and projectiles!"

CHAPTER XVIII
IN A STORM

Surprise, for the moment, held Mr. Damon, Ned and Lieutenant Marbury speechless. They looked from the heaving waters of the ocean below them to the young pilot of the Mars. He smiled at their astonishment.

"What—what does it mean, Tom?" asked Ned. "You never said you were going to take a trip as far as this."

"That's right," chimed in Mr. Damon. "Bless my nightcap! If I had known I was going to be brought so far away from home I'd never have come."

"You're not so very far from Waterford," put in Tom. "We didn't make any kind of speed coming from Shopton, and we could be back again inside of four hours if we had to."

"Then you didn't travel fast during the night?" asked the government man.

"No, we just drifted along," Tom answered. "I gave orders to run the machinery slowly, as I wanted to get it in good shape for the other tests that will come soon. But I told George, whom I left in charge when I turned in, to head for New York. I wanted to get out over the ocean to try the guns with the new recoil arrangement."

"Well, we're over the ocean all right," spoke Ned, as he looked down at the heaving waters.

"It isn't the first time," replied Tom cheerfully. "Koku, you may serve breakfast now," for the giant had been taken along as a sort of cook and waiter. Koku manifested no surprise or alarm when he found the airship floating over the sea. Whatever Tom did was right to him. He had great confidence in his master.

"No, it isn't the first time we've taken a water flight," spoke Ned. "I was only surprised at the suddenness of it, that's all."

"It's my first experience so far out above the water," observed Lieutenant Marbury, "though of course I've sailed on many seas. Why, we're out of sight of land."

"About ten miles out, yes," admitted Tom. "Far enough to make it safe to test the guns with real projectiles. That is what I want to do."

"And we've been running all night?" asked Mr. Damon.

"Yes, but at slow speed. The engines are in better shape now than ever before," Tom said. "Well, if you're ready we'll have breakfast."

The meal was served by Koku with as much unconcern as though they were in the Swift homestead back in Shopton, instead of floating near the clouds. And while it was being eaten in the main cabin, and while the crew was having breakfast in their quarters, the aerial warship was moving along over the ocean in charge of George Watson, one of Tom's engineers, who was stationed in the forward pilot-house.

"So you're going to give the guns a real test this time, is that it, Tom?" asked Ned, as he pushed back his plate, a signal that he had eaten enough.

"That's about it."

"But don't you think it's a bit risky out over the water this way. Supposing something should—should happen?" Ned hesitated.

"You mean we might fall?" asked Tom, with a smile.

"Yes; or turn upside down."

"Nothing like that could happen. I'm so sure that I have solved the problem of the recoil of the guns that I'm willing to take chances. But if any of you want to get off the Mars while the test is being made, I have a small boat I can lower, and let you row about in that until—"

"No, thank you!" interrupted Mr. Damon, as he looked below. There was quite a heavy swell on, and the ocean did not appear very attractive. They would be much more comfortable in the big Mars.

"I think you won't have any trouble," asserted Lieutenant Marbury. "I believe Tom Swift has the right idea about the guns, and there will be so small a shock from the recoil that it will not be noticeable."

"We'll soon know," spoke Tom. "I'm going to get ready for the test now."

They were now well out from shore, over the Atlantic, but to make certain no ships would be endangered by the projectiles, Tom and the others searched the waters to the horizon with powerful glasses. Nothing was seen and the work of loading the guns was begun. The bomb tubes, in the main cabin, were also to be given a test.

As service charges were to be used, and as the projectiles were filled with explosives, great care was needed in handling them.

"We'll try dropping bombs first," Tom suggested. "We know they will work, and that will be so much out of the way."

To make the test a severe one, small floating targets were first dropped overboard from the Mars. Then the aerial warship, circling about, came on toward them. Tom, seated at the range-finders, pressed the button that released the shells containing the explosives. One after another they dropped into the sea, exploding as they fell, and sending up a great column of salt water.

"Every one a hit!" reported Lieutenant Marbury, who was keeping "score."

"That's good," responded Tom. "But the others won't be so easy. We have nothing to shoot at."

They had to fire the other guns without targets at which to aim. But, after all, it was the absence of recoil they wanted to establish, and this could be done without shooting at any particular object.

One after another the guns were loaded. As has been explained, they were now made double, one barrel carrying the projectile, and the other a charge of water.

"Are you ready?" asked Tom, when it was time to fire. Lieutenant Marbury, Ned and Mr. Damon were helping, by being stationed at the pressure gauges to note the results.

"All ready," answered Ned.

"Do you think we'd better put on life preservers, Tom?" asked Mr. Damon.

"Nonsense! What for?"

"In case—in case anything happens."

"Nothing will happen. Look out now, I'm going to fire."

The guns were to be fired simultaneously by means of an electric current, when Tom pressed a button.

"Here they go!" exclaimed the young inventor.

There was a moment of waiting, and then came a thundering roar. The Mars trembled, but she did not shift to either side from an even keel. From one barrel of the guns shot out the explosive projectiles, and from the other spurted a jet of water, sent out by a charge of powder, equal in weight to that which forced out the shot.

As the projectile was fired in one direction, and the water in one directly opposite, the two discharges neutralized one another.

Out flew the pointed steel shells, to fall harmlessly into the sea, where they exploded, sending up columns of water.

"Well!" cried Tom as the echoes died away. "How was it?"

"Couldn't have been better," declared Lieutenant Marbury. "There wasn't the least shock of recoil. Tom Swift, you have solved the problem, I do believe! Your aerial warship is a success!"

"I'm glad to hear you say so. There are one or two little things that need changing, but I really think I have about what the United States Government wants."

"I am, also, of that belief, Tom. If only—" The officer stopped suddenly.

"Well?" asked Tom suggestively.

"I was going to say if only those foreign spies don't make trouble."

"I think we've seen the last of them," Tom declared. "Now we'll go on with the tests."

More guns were fired, singly and in batteries, and in each case the Mars stood the test perfectly. The double barrel had solved the recoil problem.

For some little time longer they remained out over the sea, going through some evolutions to test the rudder control, and then as their present object had been accomplished Tom gave orders to head back to Shopton, which place was reached in due time.

"Well, Tom, how was it?" asked Mr. Swift, for though his son had said nothing to his friends about the prospective test, the aged inventor knew about it.

"Successful, Dad, in every particular."

"That's good. I didn't think you could do it. But you did. I tell you it isn't much that can get the best of a Swift!" exclaimed the aged man proudly. "Oh, by the way, Tom, here's a telegram that came while you were gone," and he handed his son the yellow envelope.

Tom ripped it open with a single gesture, and in a flash his eyes took in the words. He read:

"Look out for spies during trial flights."

The message was signed with a name Tom did not recognize.

"Any bad news?" asked Mr. Swift.

"No—oh, no," replied Tom, as he crumpled up the paper and thrust it into his pocket. "No bad news, Dad."

"Well, I'm glad to hear that," went on Mr. Swift. "I don't like telegrams."

When Tom showed the message to Lieutenant Marbury, that official, after one glance at the signature, said:

"Pierson, eh? Well, when he sends out a warning it generally means something."

"Who's Pierson?" asked Tom.

"Head of the Secret Service department that has charge of this airship matter. There must be something in the wind, Tom."

Extra precautions were taken about the shops. Strangers were not permitted to enter, and all future work on the Mars was kept secret. Nevertheless, Tom was worried. He did not want his work to be spoiled just when it was about to be a success. For that it was a success, Lieutenant Marbury assured him. The government man said he would have no hesitation in recommending the purchase of Tom's aerial warship.

"There's just one other test I want to see made," he said.

"What is that?" Tom inquired.

"In a storm. You know we can't always count on having good weather, and I'd like to see how she behaves in a gale."

"You shall!" declared the young inventor.

For the next week, during which finishing touches were put on the big craft, Tom anxiously waited for signs of a storm. At last they came. Danger signals were put up all along the coast, and warnings were sent out broadcast by the Weather Bureau at Washington.

One dull gray morning Tom roused his friends early and announced that the Mars was going up.

"A big storm is headed this way," Tom said, "and we'll have a chance to see how she behaves in it."

And even as the flight began, the forerunning wind and rain came in a gust of fury. Into the midst of it shot the big aerial warship, with her powerful propellers beating the moisture-laden air.

CHAPTER XIX
QUEER HAPPENINGS

"Say, Tom, are you sure you're all right?"

"Of course I am! What do you mean?"

It was Ned Newton who asked the question, and Tom Swift who answered it. The chums were in the pilot-house of the dipping, swaying Mars, which was nosing her way into the storm, fighting on an upward slant, trying, if possible, to get above the area of atmospheric disturbance.

"Well, I mean are you sure your craft will stand all this straining, pulling and hauling?" went on Ned, as he clung to a brass hand rail, built in the side of the pilot-house wall for the very purpose to which it was now being put.

"If she doesn't stand it she's no good!" cried Tom, as he clung to the steering wheel, which was nearly torn from his hands by the deflections of the rudders.

"Well, it's taking a big chance, it seems to me," went on Ned, as he peered through the rain-spotted bull's-eyes of the pilot-house.

"There's no danger," declared Tom. "I wanted to give the ship the hardest test possible before I formally offered her to the government. If she can't stand a blow like this she isn't what I thought her, and I'll have to build another. But I'm sure she will stand the racket, Ned. She's built strongly, and even if part of the gas bag is carried away, as it was when our propeller shattered, we can still sail. If you think this is anything, wait until we turn about and begin to fight our way against the wind."

"Are you going to do that, Tom?"

"I certainly am. We're going with the gale now, to see what is the highest rate of speed we can attain. Pretty soon I'm going to turn her around, and see if she can make any headway in the other direction. Of course I know she won't make much, if any speed, against the gale; but I must give her that test."

"Well, Tom, you know best, of course," admitted Ned. "But to me it seems like taking a big risk."

And indeed it did seem, not only to Ned, but to some of the experienced men of Tom's crew, that the young inventor was taking more chances than ever before, and Tom, as my old readers well know, had, in his career, taken some big ones.

The storm grew worse as the day progressed, until it was a veritable hurricane of wind and rain. The warnings of the Weather Bureau had not been exaggerated. But through the fierce blow the Mars fought her way. As Tom had said, she was going with the wind. This was comparatively easy. But what would happen when she headed into the storm?

Mr. Damon, in the main cabin, sat and looked at Lieutenant Marbury, the eccentric man now and then blessing something as he happened to think of it.

"Do you—do you think we are in any danger?" he finally asked.

"Not at present," replied the government expert.

"You mean we will be—later?"

"It's hard to say. I guess Tom Swift knows his business, though."

"Bless my accident insurance policy!" murmured Mr. Damon. "I wish I had stayed home. If my wife ever hears of this—" He did not seem able to finish the sentence.

In the engine-room the crew were busy over the various machines. Some of the apparatus was being strained to keep the ship on her course in the powerful wind, and would be under a worse stress when Tom turned his craft about. But, so far, nothing had given way, and everything was working smoothly.

As hour succeeded hour and nothing happened, the timid ones aboard began to take more courage. Tom never for a moment lost heart. He knew what his craft could do, and he had taken her up in a terrific storm with a definite purpose in view. He was the calmest person aboard, with the exception, perhaps, of Koku. The giant did not seem to know what fear was. He depended entirely on Tom, and as long as his young master had charge of matters the giant was content to obey orders.

There was to be no test of the guns this time. They had worked sufficiently well, and, if need be, could have been fired in the gale. But Tom did not want his men to take unnecessary risks, nor was he foolhardy himself.

"We'll have our hands full when we turn around and head into the wind," he said to his chum. "That will be enough."

"Then you're really going to give the Mars that test?"

"I surely am. I don't want any comebacks from Uncle Sam after he accepts my aerial warship. I've guaranteed that she'll stand up and make headway against a gale, and I'm going to prove it."

Lieutenant Marbury was told of the coming trial, and he prepared to take official note of it. While matters were being gotten in readiness Tom turned the wheel over to his assistant pilot and went to the engine-room to see that everything was in good shape to cope with any emergency. The rudders had been carefully examined before the flight was made, to make sure they would not fail, for on them depended the progress of the ship against the powerful wind.

"I rather guess those foreign spies have given up trying to do Tom an injury," remarked Ned to the lieutenant as they sat in the main cabin, listening to the howl of the wind, and the dash of the rain.

"Well, I certainly hope so," was the answer. "But I wouldn't be too sure. The folks in Washington evidently think something is likely to happen, or they wouldn't have sent that warning telegram."

"But we haven't seen anything of the spies," Ned remarked.

"No, but that isn't any sign they are not getting ready to make trouble. This may be the calm before the storm. Tom must still be on the lookout. It isn't as though his inventions alone were in danger, for they would not hesitate to inflict serious personal injury if their plans were thwarted."

"They must be desperate."

"They are. But here comes Tom now. He looks as though something new was about to happen."

"Take care of yourselves now," advised the young aero-inventor, as he entered the cabin, finding it hard work to close the door against the terrific wind pressure.

"Why?" asked Ned.

"Because we are going to turn around and fight our way back against the gale. We may be turned topsy-turvy for a second or two."

"Bless my shoe-horn!" cried Mr. Damon. "Do you mean upside down, Tom?"

"No, not that exactly. But watch out!"

Tom went forward to the pilot-house, followed by Ned and the lieutenant. The latter wanted to take official note of what happened. Tom relieved the man at the wheel, and gradually began to alter the direction of the craft.

At first no change was noticeable. So strong was the force of the wind that it seemed as though the Mars was going in the same direction. But Ned, noticing a direction compass on the wall, saw that the needle was gradually shifting.

"Hold fast!" cried Tom suddenly. Then with a quick shift of the rudder something happened. It seemed as though the Mars was trying to turn over, and slide along on her side, or as if she wanted to turn about and scud before the gale, instead of facing it. But Tom held her to the reverse course.

"Can you get her around?" cried the lieutenant above the roar of the gale.

"I—I'm going to!" muttered Tom through his set teeth.

Inch by inch he fought the big craft through the storm. Inch by inch the indicator showed the turning, until at last the grip of the gale was overcome.

"Now she's headed right into it!" cried Tom in exultation. "She's nosing right into it!"

And the Mars was. There was no doubt of it. She had succeeded, under Tom's direction, in changing squarely about, and was now going against the wind, instead of with it.

"But we can't expect to make much speed," Tom said, as he signaled for more power, for he had lowered it somewhat in making the turn.

But Tom himself scarcely had reckoned on the force of his craft, for as the propellers whirled more rapidly the aerial warship did begin to make headway, and that in the teeth of a terrific wind.

"She's doing it, Tom! She's doing it!" cried Ned exultingly.

"I believe she is," agreed the lieutenant.

"Well, so much the better," Tom said, trying to be calm. "If she can keep this up a little while I'll give her a rest and we'll go up above the storm area, and beat back home."

The Mars, so far, had met every test. Tom had decided on ten minutes more of gale-fighting, when from the tube that communicated with the engine-room came a shrill whistle.

"See what that is, Ned," Tom directed.

"Yes," called Ned into the mouthpiece. "What's the matter?"

"Short circuit in the big motor," was the reply. "We've got to run on storage battery. Send Tom back here! Something queer has happened!"

CHAPTER XX
THE STOWAWAYS

Ned repeated the message breathlessly.

"Short circuit!" gasped Tom. "Run on storage battery! I'll have to see to that. Take the wheel somebody!"

"Wouldn't it be better to turn about, and run before the wind, so as not to put too great a strain on the machinery?" asked Lieutenant Marbury.

"Perhaps," agreed Tom. "Hold her this way, though, until I see what's wrong!"

Ned and the government man took the wheel, while Tom hurried along the runway leading from the pilot-house to the machinery cabin. The gale was still blowing fiercely.

The young inventor cast a hasty look about the interior of the place as he entered. He sniffed the air suspiciously, and was aware of the odor of burning insulation.

"What happened?" he asked, noting that already the principal motive power was coming from the big storage battery. The shift had been made automatically, when the main motor gave out.

"It's hard to say," was the answer of the chief engineer. "We were running along all right, and we got your word to switch on more power, after the turn. We did that all right, and she was running as smooth as a sewing-machine, when, all of a sudden, she short-circuited, and the storage battery cut in automatically."

"Think you put too heavy a load on the motor?" Tom asked.

"Couldn't have been that. The shunt box would have taken that up, and the circuit-breaker would have worked, saving us a burn-out, and that's what happened—a burn-out. The motor will have to be rewound."

"Well, no use trying to fight this gale with the storage battery," Tom said, after a moment's thought. "We'll run before it. That's the easiest way. Then we'll try to rise above the wind."

He sent the necessary message to the pilot-house. A moment later the shift was made, and once more the Mars was scudding before the storm. Then Tom gave his serious attention to what had happened in the engine room.

As he bent over the burned-out motor, looking at the big shiny connections, he saw something that startled him. With a quick motion Tom Swift picked up a bar of copper. It was hot to the touch—so hot that he dropped it with a cry of pain, though he had let go so quickly that the burn was only momentary.

"What's the matter?" asked Jerry Mound, Tom's engineer.

"Matter!" cried Tom. "A whole lot is the matter! That copper bar is what made the short circuit. It's hot yet from the electric current. How did it fall on the motor connections?"

The engine room force gathered about the young inventor. No one could explain how the copper bar came to be where it was. Certainly no one of Tom's employees had put it there, and it could not have fallen by accident, for the motor connections were protected by a mesh of wire, and a hand would have to be thrust under them to put the bar in place. Tom gave a quick look at his men. He knew he could trust them—every one. But this was a queer happening.

For a moment Tom did not know what to think, and then, as the memory of that warning telegram came to him, he had an idea.

"Were any strangers in this cabin before the start was made?" he asked Mr. Mound.

"Not that I know of," was the answer.

"Well, there may be some here now," Tom said grimly. "Look about."

But a careful search revealed no one. Yet the young inventor was sure the bar of copper, which had done the mischief of short-circuiting the motor, had been put in place deliberately.

In reality there was no danger to the craft, since there was power enough in the storage battery to run it for several hours. But the happening showed Tom he had still to reckon with his enemies.

He looked at the height gauge on the wall of the motor-room, and noted that the Mars was going up. In accordance with Tom's instructions they were sending her above the storm area. Once there, with no gale to fight, they could easily beat their way back to a point above Shopton, and make the best descent possible.

And that was done while, under Tom's direction, his men took the damaged motor apart, with a view to repairing it.

"What was it, Tom?" asked Ned, coming back to join his chum, after George Ventor, the assistant pilot, had taken charge of the wheel.

"I don't exactly know, Ned," was the answer. "But I feel certain that some of my enemies came aboard here and worked this mischief."

"Your enemies came aboard?"

"Yes, and they must be here now. The placing of that copper bar proves it."

"Then let's make a search and find them, Tom. It must be some of those foreign spies."

"Just what I think."

But a more careful search of the craft than the one Tom had casually made revealed the presence of no one. All the crew and helpers were accounted for, and, as they had been in Tom's service for some time, they were beyond suspicion. Yet the fact remained that a seemingly human agency had acted to put the main motor out of commission. Tom could not understand it.

"Well, it sure is queer," observed Ned, as the search came to nothing.

"It's worse than queer," declared Tom, "it's alarming! I don't know when I'll be safe if we have ghosts aboard."

"Ghosts?" repeated Ned.

"Well, when we can't find out who put that bar in place I might as well admit it was a ghost," spoke Tom. "Certainly, if it was done by a man, he didn't jump overboard after doing it, and he isn't here now. It sure is queer!"

Ned agreed with the last statement, at any rate.

In due time the Mars, having fought her way above the storm, came over Shopton, and then, the wind having somewhat died out, she fought her way down, and, after no little trouble, was housed in the hangar.

Tom cautioned his friends and workmen to say nothing to his father about the mysterious happening on board.

"I'll just tell him we had a slight accident, and let it go at that," Tom decided. "No use in causing him worry."

"But what are you going to do about it?" asked Ned.

"I'm going to keep careful watch over the aerial warship, at any rate," declared Tom. "If there's a hidden enemy aboard, I'll starve him out."

Accordingly, a guard, under the direction of Koku, was posted about the big shed, but nothing came of it. No stranger was observed to sneak out of the ship, after it had been deserted by the crew. The mystery seemed deeper than ever.

It took nearly a week to repair the big motor, and, during this time, Tom put some improvements on the airship, and added the finishing touches.

He was getting it ready for the final government test, for the authorities in Washington had sent word that they would have Captain Warner, in addition to Lieutenant Marbury, make the final inspection and write a report.

Meanwhile several little things occurred to annoy Tom. He was besieged with applications from new men who wanted to work, and many of these men seemed to be foreigners. Tom was sure they were either spies of some European nations, or the agents of spies, and they got no further than the outer gate.

But some strangers did manage to sneak into the works, though they were quickly detected and sent about their business. Also, once or twice, small fires were discovered in outbuildings, but they were soon extinguished with little damage. Extra vigilance was the watchword.

"And yet, with all my precautions, they may get me, or damage something," declared Tom. "It is very annoying!"

"It is," agreed Ned, "and we must be doubly on the lookout."

So impressed was Ned with the necessity for caution that he arranged to take his vacation at this time, so as to be on hand to help his chum, if necessary.

The Mars was nearing completion. The repaired motor was better than ever, and everything was in shape for the final test. Mr. Damon was persuaded to go along, and Koku was to be taken, as well as the two government officials.

The night before the trip the guards about the airship shed were doubled, and Tom made two visits to the place before midnight. But there was no alarm.

Consequently, when the Mars started off on her final test, it was thought that all danger from the spies was over.

"She certainly is a beauty," said Captain Warner, as the big craft shot upward. "I shall be interested in seeing how she stands gun fire, though."

"Oh, she'll stand it," declared Lieutenant Marbury. The trip was to consume several days of continuous flying, to test the engines. A large supply of food and ammunition was aboard.

It was after supper of the first day out, and our friends were seated in the main cabin laying out a program for the next day, when sudden yells came from a part of the motor cabin devoted to storage. Koku, who had been sent to get out a barrel of oil, was heard to shout.

"What's up?" asked Tom, starting to his feet. He was answered almost at once by more yells.

"Oh, Master! Come quickly!" cried the giant. "There are many men here. There are stowaways aboard!"

CHAPTER XXI
PRISONERS

For a moment, after hearing Koku's reply, neither Tom nor his friends spoke. Then Ned, in a dazed sort of way, repeated:

"Stowaways!"

"Bless my—" began Mr. Damon, but that was as far as he got.

From the engine compartment, back of the amidship cabin, came a sound of cries and heavy blows. The yells of Koku could be heard above those of the others.

Then the door of the cabin where Tom Swift and his friends were was suddenly burst open, and seven or eight men threw themselves within. They were led by a man with a small, dark mustache and a little tuft of whiskers on his chin—an imperial. He looked the typical Frenchman, and his words, snapped out, bore out that belief.

What he said was in French, as Tom understood, though he knew little of that language. Also, what the Frenchman said produced an immediate result, for the men following him sprang at our friends with overwhelming fierceness.

Before Tom, Ned, Captain Warner, Mr. Damon or Lieutenant Marbury could grasp any weapon with which to defend themselves, had their intentions been to do so, they were seized.

Against such odds little could be done, though our friends did not give up without a struggle.

"What does this mean?" angrily demanded Tom Swift. "Who are you? What are you doing aboard my craft? Who are—"

His words were lost in smothered tones, for one of his assailants put a heavy cloth over his mouth, and tied it there, gagging him. Another man, with a quick motion, whipped a rope about Tom's hands and feet, and he was soon securely bound.

In like manner the others were treated, and, despite the struggles of Mr. Damon, the two government men and Ned, they were soon put in a position where they could do nothing—helplessly bound, and laid on a bench in the main cabin, staring blankly up at the ceiling. Each one was gagged so effectively that he could not utter more than a faint moan.

Of the riot of thoughts that ran through the heads of each one, I leave you to imagine.

What did it all mean? Where had the strange men come from? What did they mean by thus assaulting Tom and his companions? And what had happened to the others of the crew—Koku, Jerry Mound, the engineer, and George Ventor, the assistant pilot?

These were only a few of the questions Tom asked himself, as he lay there, bound and helpless. Doubtless Mr. Damon and the others were asking themselves similar questions.

One thing was certain—whatever the stowaways, as Koku had called them, had done, they had not neglected the Mars, for she was running along at about the same speed, though in what direction Tom could not tell. He strained to get a view of the compass on the forward wall of the cabin, but he could not see it.

It had been a rough-and-tumble fight, by which our friends were made prisoners, but no one seemed to have been seriously, or even slightly, hurt. The invaders, under the leadership of the Frenchman, were rather ruffled, but that was all.

Pantingly they stood in line, surveying their captives, while the man with the mustache and imperial smiled in a rather superior fashion at the row of bound ones. He spoke in his own tongue to the men, who, with the exception of one, filed out, going, as Tom and the others could note, to the engine-room in the rear.

"I hope I have not had to hurt any of you," the Frenchman observed, with sarcastic politeness. "I regret the necessity that caused me to do this, but, believe me, it was unavoidable."

He spoke with some accent, and Tom at once decided this was the same man who had once approached Eradicate. He also recognized him as the man he had seen in the woods the day of the outing.

"He's one of the foreign spies," thought Tom "and he's got us and the ship, too. They were too many for us!"

Tom's anxiety to speak, to hold some converse with the captor, was so obvious that the Frenchman said:

"I am going to treat you as well as I can under the circumstances. You and your other friends, who are also made prisoners, will be allowed to be together, and then you can talk to your hearts' content."

The other man, who had remained with the evident ringleader of the stowaways, asked a question, in French, and he used the name La Foy.

"Ah!" thought Tom. "This is the leader of the gang that attacked Koku in the shop that night. They have been waiting their chance, and now they have made good. But where did they come from? Could they have boarded us from some other airship?"

Yet, as Tom asked himself that question, he knew it could hardly have been possible. The men must have been in hiding on his own craft, they must have been, as Koku had cried out—stowaways—and have come out at a preconcerted signal to overpower the aviators.

"If you will but have patience a little longer," went on La Foy, for that was evidently the name of the leader, "you will all be together. We are just considering where best to put you so that you will not suffer too much. It is quite a problem to deal with so many prisoners, but we have no choice."

The two Frenchmen conversed rapidly in their own language for a few minutes, and then there came into the cabin another of the men who had helped overpower Tom and his friends. What he told La Foy seemed to give that individual satisfaction, for he smiled.

"We are going to put you all together in the largest storeroom, which is partly empty," La Foy said. "There you will be given food and drink, and treated as well as possible under the circumstances. You will also be unbound, and may converse among yourselves. I need hardly point out," he went on, "that calling for help will be useless. We are a mile or so in the air, and have no intention of descending," and he smiled mockingly.

"They must know how to navigate my aerial warship," thought Tom. "I wonder what their game is, anyhow?"

Night had fallen, but the cabin was aglow with electric lights. The foreigners in charge of the Mars seemed to know their way about perfectly, and how to manage the big craft. By the vibration Tom could tell that the motor was running evenly and well.

"But what happened to the others—to Mound, Ventor and Koku?" wondered Tom.

A moment later several of the foreigners entered. Some of them did not look at all like Frenchmen, and Tom was sure one was a German and another a Russian.

"This will be your prison—for a while," said La Foy significantly, and Tom wondered how long this would be the case. A sharp thought came to him—how long would they be prisoners? Did not some other, and more terrible, fate await them?

As La Foy spoke, he opened a storeroom door that led off from the main, or amidship, cabin. This room was intended to contain the supplies and stores that would be taken on a long voyage. It was one of two, being the larger, and now contained only a few odds and ends of little importance. It made a strong prison, as Tom well knew, having planned it.

One by one, beginning with Tom, the prisoners were taken up and placed in a recumbent position on the floor of the storeroom. Then were brought in the engineer and assistant pilot, as well as Koku and a machinist whom Tom had brought along to help him. Now the young inventor and all his friends were together. It took four men to carry Koku in, the giant being covered with a network of ropes.

"On second thought," said La Foy, as he saw Koku being placed with his friends, "I think we will keep the big man with us. We had trouble enough to subdue him. Carry him back to the engine-room."

So Koku, trussed up like some roped steer, was taken out again.

"Now then," said La Foy to his prisoners, as he stood in the door of the room, "I will unbind one of you, and he may loose the bonds of the others."

As he spoke, he took the rope from Tom's hands, and then, quickly slipping out, locked and barred the door.

CHAPTER XXII
APPREHENSIONS

For a moment or two, after the ropes binding his hands were loosed, Tom Swift did nothing. He was not only stunned mentally, but the bonds had been pulled so tightly about his wrists that the circulation was impeded, and his cramped muscles required a little time in which to respond.

But presently he felt the tingle of the coursing blood, and he found he could move his arms. He raised them to his head, and then his first care was to remove the pad of cloth that formed a gag over his mouth. Now he could talk.

"I—I'll loosen you all in just a second," he said, as he bent over to pick at the knot of the rope around his legs. His own voice sounded strange to him.

"I don't know what it's all about, any more than you do," he went on, speaking to the others. "It's a fierce game we're up against, and we've got to make the best of it. As soon as we can move, and talk, we'll decide what's best to do. Whoever these fellows are, and I believe they are the foreign spies I've been warned about, they are in complete possession of the airship."

Tom found it no easy matter to loosen the bonds on his feet. The ropes were well tied, and Tom's fingers were stiff from the lack of circulation of blood. But finally he managed to free himself. When he stood up in the dim storeroom, that was now a prison for all save Koku, he found that he could not walk. He almost toppled over, so weak were his legs from the tightness of the ropes. He sat down and worked his muscles until they felt normal again.

A few minutes later, weak and rather tottery, he managed to reach Mr. Damon, whom he first unbound. He realized that Mr. Damon was the oldest of his friends, and, consequently, would suffer most. And it was characteristic of the eccentric gentleman that, as soon as his gag was removed he burst out with:

"Bless my wristlets, Tom! What does it all mean?"

"That's more than I can say, Mr. Damon," replied Tom, with a mournful shake of his head. "I'm very sorry it happened, for it looks as though I hadn't taken proper care. The idea of those men stowing themselves away on board here, and me not knowing it; and then coming out unexpectedly and getting possession of the craft! It doesn't speak very well for my smartness."

"Oh, well, Tom, anyone might have been fooled by those plotting foreigners," said Mr. Damon. "Now, we'll try to turn matters about and get the best of them. Oh, but it feels good to be free once more!"

He stretched his benumbed and stiffened limbs and then helped Tom free the others. They stood up, looking at each other in their dimly lighted prison.

"Well, if this isn't the limit I don't know what is!" cried Ned Newton.

"They got the best of you, Tom," spoke Lieutenant Marbury.

"Are they really foreign spies?" asked Captain Warner.

"Yes," replied his assistant. "They managed to carry out the plot we tried to frustrate. It was a good trick, too, hiding on board, and coming out with a rush."

"Is that what they did?" asked Mr. Damon.

"It looks so," observed Tom. "The attack must have started in the engine-room," he went on, with a look at Mound and Ventor. "What happened there?" he asked.

"Well, that's about the way it was," answered the engineer. "We were working away, making some adjustments, oiling the parts and seeing that everything was running smoothly, when, all at once, I heard Koku yell. He had gone in the oil room. At first I thought something had gone wrong with the ship, but, when I looked at the giant, I saw he was being attacked by four strange men. And, before I, or any of the other men, could do anything, they all swarmed down on us.

"There must have been a dozen of them, and they simply overwhelmed us. One of them hit Koku on the head with an iron bar, and that took all the fight out of the giant, or the story might have been a different one. As it was, we were overpowered, and that's all I know until we were carried in here, and saw you folks all tied up as we were."

"They burst in on us in the same way," Tom explained. "But where did they come from? Where were they hiding?"

"In the oil and gasoline storeroom that opens out of the motor compartment," answered Mound, the engineer. "It isn't half full, you know, and there's room for more than a dozen men in it. They must have gone in some time last night, when the airship was in the hangar, and remained hidden among the boxes and barrels until they got ready to come out and overpower us."

"That's it," decided Tom. "But I don't understand how they got in. The hangar was well guarded all night."

"Some of your men might have been bribed," suggested Ned.

"Yes, that is so," admitted Tom, and, later, he learned that such had been the case. The foreign spies, for such they were, had managed to corrupt one of Tom's trusted employees, who had looked the other way when La Foy and his fellow-conspirators sneaked into the airship shed and secreted themselves.

"Well, discussing how they got on board isn't going to do us any good now," Tom remarked ruefully. "The question is—what are we going to do?"

"Bless my fountain pen!" cried Mr. Damon. "There's only one thing to do!"

"What is that?" asked Ned.

"Why, get out of here, call a policeman, and have these scoundrels arrested. I'll prosecute them! I'll have my lawyer on hand to see that they get the longest terms the statutes call for! Bless my pocketbook, but I will!" and Mr. Damon waxed quite indignant.

"That's easier said than done," observed Tom Swift, quietly. "In the first place, it isn't going to be an easy matter to get out of here."

He looked around the storeroom, which was then their prison. It was illuminated by a single electric light, which showed some boxes and barrels piled in the rear.

"Nothing in them to help us get out," Tom went on, for he knew what the contents were.

"Oh, we'll get out," declared Ned confidently, "but I don't believe we'll find a policeman ready to take our complaint. The upper air isn't very well patrolled as yet."

"That's so," agreed Mr. Damon. "I forgot that we were in an airship. But what is to be done, Tom? We really are captives aboard our own craft."

"Yes, worse luck," returned the young inventor. "I feel foolish when I think how we let them take us prisoners."

"We couldn't help it," Ned commented. "They came on us too suddenly. We didn't have a chance. And they outnumbered us two to one. If they could take care of big Koku, what chance did we have?"

"Very little," said Engineer Mound. "They were desperate fellows. They know something about aircraft, too. For, as soon as Koku, Ventor and I were disposed of, some of them went at the machinery as if they had been used to running it all their lives."

"Oh, the foreigners are experts when it comes to craft of the air," said Captain Warner.

"Well, they seem to be running her, all right," admitted the young inventor, "and at good speed, too. They have increased our running rate, if I am any judge."

"By several miles an hour," confirmed the assistant pilot. "Though in which direction they are heading, and what they are going to do with us is more than I can guess."

"That's so!" agreed Mr. Damon. "What is to become of us? They may heave us overboard into the ocean!"

"Into the ocean!" cried Ned apprehensively. "Are we near the sea?"

"We must be, by this time," spoke Tom. "We were headed in that direction, and we have come almost far enough to put us somewhere over the Atlantic, off the Jersey coast."

A look of apprehension was on the faces of all. But Tom's face did not remain clouded long.

"We won't try to swim until we have to," he said. "Now, let's take an account of stock, and see if we have any means of getting out of this prison."

CHAPTER XXIII
ACROSS THE SEA

With one accord the hands of the captives sought their pockets. Probably the first thought of each one was a knife—a pocket knife. But blank looks succeeded their first hopeful ones, for the hands came out empty.

"Not a thing!" exclaimed Mr. Damon. "Not a blessed thing! They have even taken my keys and—my fountain pen!"

"I guess they searched us all while they were struggling with us, tying us up," suggested Ned. "I had a knife with a big, strong blade, but it's gone."

"So is mine," echoed Tom.

"And I haven't even a screwdriver, or a pocket-wrench," declared the engineer, "though I had both."

"They evidently knew what they were doing," said Lieutenant Marbury. "I don't usually carry a revolver, but of late I have had a small automatic in my pocket. That's gone, too."

"And so are all my things," went on his naval friend. "That Frenchman, La Foy, was taking no chances."

"Well, if we haven't any weapons, or means of getting out of here, we must make them," said Tom, as hopefully as he could under the circumstances. "I don't know all the things that were put in this storeroom, and perhaps there may be something we can use."

"Shall we make the try now?" asked Ned. "I'm getting thirsty, at least. Lucky we had supper before they came out at us."

"Well, there isn't any water in here, or anything to eat, of so much I am sure," went on Tom "So we will have to depend on our captors for that."

"At least we can shout and ask for water," said Lieutenant Marbury. "They have no excuse for being needlessly cruel."

They all agreed that this might not be a bad plan, and were preparing to raise a united shout, when there came a knock on the door of their prison.

"Are you willing to listen to reason?" asked a voice they recognized as that of La Foy.

"What do you mean by reason?" asked Tom bitterly. "You have no right to impose any conditions on us."

"I have the right of might, and I intend exercising it," was the sharp rejoinder. "If you will listen to reason—"

"Which kind—yours or ours?" asked Tom pointedly.

"Mine, in this case," snapped back the Frenchman. "What I was going to say was that I do not intend to starve you, or cause you discomfort by thirst. I am going to open the door and put in food and water. But I warn you that any attempt to escape will be met with severe measures.

"We are in sufficient force to cope with you. I think you have seen that." He spoke calmly and in perfect English, though with a marked accent. "My men are armed, and will stand here ready to meet violence with violence," he went on. "Is that understood?"

For a moment none of the captives replied.

"I think it will be better to give in to him at least for a while," said Captain Warner in a low voice to Tom. "We need water, and will soon need food. We can think and plan better if we are well nourished."

"Then you think I should promise not to raise a row?"

"For the time being—yes."

"Well, I am waiting!" came in sharp tones from the other side of the portal.

"Our answer is—yes," spoke Tom. "We will not try to get out—just yet," he added significantly.

A key was heard grating in the lock, and, a moment later, the door slid back. Through the opening could be seen La Foy and some of his men standing armed. Others had packages of food and jugs of water. A plentiful supply of the latter was carried aboard the Mars.

"Keep back from the door!" was the stern command of La Foy. "The food and drink will be passed in only if you keep away from the entrance. Remember my men are armed!"

The warning was hardly needed, for the weapons could plainly be seen. Tom had half a notion that perhaps a concerted rush would carry the day for him and his friends, but he was forced to abandon that idea.

While the guards looked on, others of the "pirate crew," as Ned dubbed them, passed in food and water. Then the door was locked again.

They all felt better after drinking the water, which was made cool by evaporation, for the airship was quite high above the earth when Tom's enemies captured it, and the young inventor felt sure it had not descended any.

No one felt much like eating, however, so the food was put away for a time. And then, somewhat refreshed, they began looking about for some means of getting out of their prison.

"Of course we might batter down the door, in time, by using some of these boxes as rams," said Tom. "But the trouble is, that would make a noise, and they could stand outside and drive us back with guns and pistols, of which they seem to have plenty."

"Yes, and they could turn some of your own quick-firers on us," added Captain Warner. "No, we must work quietly, I think, and take them unawares, as they took us. That is our only plan."

"We will be better able to see what we have here by daylight," Tom said. "Suppose we wait until morning?"

That plan was deemed best, and preparations made for spending the night in their prison.

It was a most uncomfortable night for all of them. The floor was their only bed, and their only covering some empty bags that had contained supplies. But even under these circumstances they managed to doze off fitfully.

Once they were all awakened by a violent plunging of the airship. The craft seemed to be trying to stand on her head, and then she rocked violently from side to side, nearly turning turtle. "What is it?" gasped Ned, who was lying next to Tom.

"They must be trying some violent stunts," replied the young inventor, "or else we have run into a storm."

"I think the latter is the case," observed Lieutenant Marbury.

And, as the motion of the craft kept up, though less violently, this was accepted as the explanation. Through the night the Mars flew, but whither the captives knew not.

The first gray streaks of dawn finally shone through the only window of their prison. Sore, lame and stiff, wearied in body and disturbed in mind, the captives awoke. Tom's first move was toward the window. It was high up, but, by standing on a box, he could look through it. He uttered an exclamation.

"What is it?" asked Ned, swaying to and fro from the violent motion of the aerial warship.

"We are away out over the sea," spoke Tom, "and in the midst of a bad storm."

CHAPTER XXIV
THE LIGHTNING BOLT

Tom turned away from the window, to find his companions regarding him anxiously.

"A storm," repeated Ned. "What sort?"

"It might turn into any sort," replied Tom. "All I can see now is a lot of black clouds, and the wind must be blowing pretty hard, for there's quite a sea on."

"Bless my galvanometer!" cried Mr. Damon. "Then we are out over the ocean again, Tom?"

"Yes, there's no doubt of it."

"What part?" asked the assistant pilot.

"That's more than I can tell," Tom answered.

"Suppose I take a look?" suggested Captain Warner. "I've done quite a bit of sailing in my time."

But, when he had taken a look through the window at which Tom had been standing, the naval officer descended, shaking his head.

"There isn't a landmark in sight," he announced. "We might be over the middle of the Atlantic, for all I could tell."

"Hardly as far as that," spoke Tom. "They haven't been pushing the Mars at that speed. But we may be across to the other side before we realize it."

"How's that?" asked Ned.

"Well, the ship is in the possession of these foreign spies," went on Tom. "All their interests are in Europe, though it would be hard to say what nationality is in command here. I think there are even some Englishmen among those who attacked us, as well as French, Germans, Italians and Russians."

"Yes, it seems to be a combination of European nations against us," admitted Captain Warner. "Probably, after they have made good their seizure of Tom's aerial warship, they will portion her out among themselves, or use her as a model from which to make others."

"Do you think that is their object?" asked Mr. Damon.

"Undoubtedly," was the captain's answer. "It has been the object of these foreign spies, all along, not only to prevent the United States from enjoying the benefits of these progressive inventions, but to use them for themselves. They would stop at nothing to gain their ends. It seems we did not sufficiently appreciate their power and daring."

"Well, they've got us, at any rate," observed Tom, "and they may take us and the ship to some far-off foreign country."

"If they don't heave us overboard half-way there," commented Ned, in rather gloomy tones.

"Well, of course, there's that possibility," admitted Tom. "They are desperate characters."

"Well, we must do something," declared Lieutenant Marbury. "Come, it's daylight now, and we can see to work better. Let's see if we can't find a way to get out of this prison. Say, but this sure is a storm!" he cried, as the airship rolled and pitched violently.

"They are handling her well, though," observed Tom, as the craft came quickly to an even keel. "Either they have a number of expert birdmen on board, or they can easily adapt themselves to a new aircraft. She is sailing splendidly."

"Well, let's eat something, and set to work," proposed Ned.

They brought out the food which had been given to them the night before, but before they could eat this, there came a knock on the door, and more food and fresh water was handed in, under the same precautions as before.

Tom and his companions indignantly demanded to be released, but their protests were only laughed at, and while the guards stood with ready weapons the door was again shut and locked.

But the prisoners were not the kind to sit idly down in the face of this. Under Tom's direction they set about looking through their place of captivity for something by which they could release themselves. At first they found nothing, and Ned even suggested trying to cut a way through the wooden walls with a fingernail file, which he found in one of his pockets, when Tom, who had gone to the far end of the storeroom, uttered a cry.

"What is it—a way out?" asked Lieutenant Marbury anxiously.

"No, but means to that end," Tom replied. "Look, a file and a saw, left here by some of my workmen, perhaps," and he brought out the tools. He had found them behind a barrel in the far end of the compartment.

"Hurray!" cried Ned. "That's the ticket! Now we'll soon show these fellows what's what!"

"Go easy!" cautioned Tom. "We must work carefully. It won't do to slam around and try to break down the door with these. I think we had better select a place on the side wall, break through that, and make an opening where we can come out unnoticed. Then, when we are ready, we can take them by surprise. We'll have to do something like that, for they outnumber us, you know."

"That is so," agreed Captain Warner. "We must use strategy."

"Well, where would be a good place to begin to burrow out?" asked Ned.

"Here," said Tom, indicating a place far back in the room. "We can work there in turns, sawing a hole through the wall. It will bring us out in the passage between the aft and amidship cabins, and we can go either way."

"Then let's begin!" cried Ned enthusiastically, and they set to work.

While the aerial warship pitched and tossed in the storm, over some part of the Atlantic, Tom and his friends took turns in working their way to freedom. With the sharp end of the file a small hole was made, the work being done as slowly as a rat gnaws, so as to make no noise that would be heard by their captors. In time the hole was large enough to admit the end of the saw.

But this took many hours, and it was not until the second day of their captivity that they had the hole nearly large enough for the passage of one person at a time. They had not been discovered, they thought.

Meanwhile they had been given food and water at intervals, but to all demands that they be released, or at least told why they were held prisoners, a deaf ear was turned.

They could only guess at the fate of Koku. Probably the giant was kept bound, for once he got the chance to use his enormous strength it might go hard with the foreigners.

The Mars continued to fly through the air. Sometimes, as Tom and his friends could tell by the motion, she was almost stationary in the upper regions, and again she seemed to be flying at top speed. Occasionally there came the sound of firing.

"They're trying my guns," observed Tom grimly.

"Do you suppose they are being attacked?" asked Ned, hopefully.

"Hardly," replied Captain Warner. "The United States possesses no craft able to cope with this one in aerial warfare, and they are hardly engaging in part of the European war yet. I think they are just trying Tom's new guns."

Later our friends learned that such was the case.

The storm had either passed, or the Mars had run out of the path of it, for, after the first few hours of pitching and tossing, the atmosphere seemed reduced to a state of calm.

All the while they were secretly working to gain their freedom so they might attack and overpower their enemies, they took occasional observations from the small window. But they could learn nothing of their whereabouts. They could only view the heaving ocean, far below them, or see a mass of cloud-mist, which hid the earth, if so be that the Mars was sailing over land.

"But how much longer can they keep it up?" asked Ned.

"Well, we have fuel and supplies aboard for nearly two weeks," Tom answered.

"And by the end of that time we may all be dead," spoke the young bank clerk despondently.

"No, we'll be out of here before then!" declared Lieutenant Marbury.

Indeed the hole was now almost large enough to enable them to crawl out one at a time. They could not, of course, see how it looked from the outside, but Tom had selected a place for its cutting so that the sawdust and the mark of the panel that was being removed, would not ordinarily be noticeable.

They set night as the time for making the attempt—late at night, when it was hoped that most of their captors would be asleep.

Finally the last cut was made, and a piece of wood hung over the opening only by a shred, all ready to knock out.

"We'll do it at midnight," announced Tom.

Anxious, indeed, were those last hours of waiting. The time had almost arrived for the attempt, when Tom, who had been nervously pacing to and fro, remarked:

"We must be running into another storm. Feel how she heaves and rolls!"

Indeed the Mars was most unsteady.

"It sure is a storm!" cried Ned, "and a heavy one, too," for there came a burst of thunder, that seemed like a report of Tom's giant cannon.

In another instant they were in the midst of a violent thunderstorm, the airship pitching and tossing in a manner to almost throw them from their feet.

As Tom reached up to switch on the electric light again, there came a flash of lightning that well nigh blinded them. And so close after it as to seem simultaneous, there came such a crash of thunder as to stun them all. There was a tingling, as of a thousand pins and needles in the body of each of the captives, and a strong smell of sulphur. Then, as the echoes of the clap died away, Tom yelled:

"She's been struck! The airship has been struck!"

CHAPTER XXV
FREEDOM

For a moment there was silence, following Tom's wild cry and the noise of the thunderclap. Then, as other, though less loud reverberations of the storm continued to sound, the captives awoke to a realization of what had happened. They had been partially stunned, and were almost as in a dream.

"Are—are we all right?" stammered Ned.

"Bless my soul! What has happened?" cried Mr. Damon.

"We've been struck by lightning!" Tom repeated. "I don't know whether we're all right or not."

"We seem to be falling!" exclaimed Lieutenant Marbury.

"If the whole gas bag isn't ripped to pieces we're lucky," commented Jerry Mound.

Indeed, it was evident that the Mars was sinking rapidly. To all there came the sensation of riding in an elevator in a skyscraper and being dropped a score of stories.

Then, as they stood there in the darkness, illuminated only by flashes from the lightning outside the window, waiting for an unknown fate, Tom Swift uttered a cry of delight.

"We've stopped falling!" he cried. "The automatic gas machine is pumping. Part of the gas bag was punctured, but the unbroken compartments hold!"

"If part of the gas leaked out I don't see why it wasn't all set on fire and exploded," observed Captain Warner.

"It's a non-burnable gas," Tom quickly explained. "But come on. This may be our very chance. There seems to be something going on that may be in our favor."

Indeed the captives could hear confused cries and the running to and fro of many feet.

He made for the sawed panel, and, in another instant, had burst out and was through it, out into the passageway between the after and amidship cabins. His companions followed him.

They looked into the rear cabin, or motor compartment, and a scene of confusion met their gaze. Two of the foreign men who had seized the ship lay stretched out on the floor near the humming machinery, which had been left to run itself. A look in the other direction, toward the main cabin, showed a group of the foreign spies bending over the inert body of La Foy, the Frenchman, stretched out on a couch.

"What has happened?" cried Ned. "What does it all mean?'

"The lightning!" exclaimed Tom. "The bolt that struck the ship has knocked out some of our enemies! Now is the time to attack them!"

The Mars seemed to have passed completely through a narrow storm belt. She was now in a quiet atmosphere, though behind her could be seen the fitful play of lightning, and there could be heard the distant rumble of thunder.

"Come on!" cried Tom. "We must act quickly, while they are demoralized! Come on!"

His friends needed no further urging. Jerry Mound and the machinist rushed to the engine-room, to look after any of the enemy that might be there, while Tom, Ned and the others ran into the middle cabin.

"Grab 'em! Tie 'em up!" cried Tom, for they had no weapons with which to make an attack.

But none were needed. So stunned were the foreigners by the lightning bolt, which had miraculously passed our friends, and so unnerved by the striking down of La Foy, their leader, that they seemed like men half asleep. Before they could offer any resistance they were bound with the same ropes that had held our friends in bondage. That is, all but the big Frenchman himself. He seemed beyond the need of binding.

Mound, the engineer, and his assistant, came hurrying in from the motor-room, followed by Koku.

"We found him chained up," Jerry explained, as the big giant, freed from his captivity, rubbed his chafed wrists.

"Are there any of the foreigners back there?'

"Only those two knocked out by the lightning," the engineer explained. "We've made them secure. I see you've got things here in shape."

"Yes," replied Tom. "And now to see where we are, and to get back home. Whew! But this has been a time! Koku, what happened to you?"

"They no let anything happen. I be in chains all the while," the giant answered. "Jump on me before I can do anything!"

"Well, you're out, now, and I think we'll have you stand guard over these men. The tables are turned, Koku."

The bound ones were carried to the same prison whence our friends had escaped, but their bonds were not taken off, and Koku was put in the place with them. By this time La Foy and the two other stricken men showed signs of returning life. They had only been stunned.

The young inventor and his friends, once more in possession of their airship, lost little time in planning to return. They found that the spies were all expert aeronauts, and had kept a careful chart of their location. They were then halfway across the Atlantic, and in a short time longer would probably have been in some foreign country. But Tom turned the Mars about.

The craft had only been slightly damaged by the lightning bolt, though three of the gas bag compartments were torn, The others sufficed, however, to make the ship sufficiently buoyant.

When morning came Tom and his friends had matters running almost as smoothly as before their capture.

The prisoners had no chance to escape, and, indeed, they seemed to have been broken in spirit. La Foy was no longer the insolent, mocking Frenchman that he had been, and the two chief foreign engineers seemed to have lost some of their reason when the lightning struck them.

"But it was a mighty lucky and narrow escape for us," said Ned, as he and Tom sat in the pilot-house the second day of the return trip.

"That's right," agreed his chum.

Once again they were above the earth, and, desiring to get rid as soon as possible of the presence of the spies, a landing was made near New York City, and the government authorities communicated with. Captain Warner and Lieutenant Marbury took charge of the prisoners, with some Secret Service men, and the foreigners were soon safely locked up.

"And now what are you going to do, Tom?" asked Ned, when, once more, they had the airship to themselves.

"I'm going back to Shopton, fix up the gas bag, and give her another government trial," was the answer.

And, in due time, this was done. Tom added some improvements to the aircraft, making it better than ever, and when she was given the test required by the government, she was an unqualified success, and the rights to the Mars were purchased for a large sum. In sailing, and in the matter of guns and bombs, Tom's craft answered every test.

"So you see I was right, after all, Dad," the young inventor said, when informed that he had succeeded. "We can shoot off even bigger guns than I thought from the deck of the Mars."

"Yes, Tom," replied the aged inventor, "I admit I was wrong."

Tom's aerial warship was even a bigger success than he had dared to hope. Once the government men fully understood how to run it, in which Tom played a prominent part in giving instructions, they put the Mars to a severe test. She was taken out over the ocean, and her guns trained on an obsolete battleship. Her bombs and projectiles blew the craft to pieces.

"The Mars will be the naval terror of the seas in any future war," predicted Captain Warner.

The Secret Service men succeeded in unearthing all the details of the plot against Tom. His life, at times, had been in danger, but at the last minute the man detailed to harm him lost his nerve.

It was Tom's enemies who had set on fire the red shed, and who later tried to destroy the ship by putting a corrosive acid in one of the propellers. That plot, though, was not wholly successful. Then came the time when one of the spies hid on board, and dropped the copper bar on the motor, short-circuiting it. But for the storage-battery that scheme might have wrought fearful damage. The spy who had stowed himself away on the craft escaped at night by the connivance of one of Tom's corrupt employees.

The foreign spies were tried and found guilty, receiving merited punishment. Of course the governments to which they belonged disclaimed any part in the seizure of Tom's aerial warship.

It came out at the trial that one of Tom's most trusted employees had proved a traitor, and had the night before the test, allowed the foreign spies to secrete themselves on board, to rush out at an opportune time to overpower our hero and his friends. But luck was with Tom at the end.

"Well, what are you going to tackle next, Tom?" asked Ned, one day about a month after these exciting experiences.

"I don't know," was the slow answer. "I think a self-swinging hammock, under an apple tree, with a never-emptying pitcher of ice-cold lemonade would be about the thing."

"Good, Tom! And, if you'll invent that, I'll share it with you."

"Well, come on, let's begin now," laughed Tom. "I need a vacation, anyhow."

But it is very much to be doubted if Tom Swift, even on a vacation, could refrain from trying to invent something, either in the line of airships, water, or land craft. And so, until he again comes to the front with something new, we will take leave of him.